THE LAST MILE OF BRAGANZA REIGN

LAMBERTO ALMEIDA

Contents

Contents

Author's Note

The characters and the stories of this novel are loosely based on author's childhood experiences, and stories of elders. The scenes and the dialogues are interpolated. This novel, except for authentic locales and historical inputs, is a work of fiction. Any resemblance to actual events or persons, living or dead, is entirely coincidental.

After initial setbacks, Afonso de Albuquerque, the Portuguese general and naval-military commander finally conquered Goa in December 1510 from the forces of Yusuf Adil Shah, the ruler of the Shahi dynasty of Bijapur.

Afonso took over as Governor of Portuguese India assuring the local leaders of a just rule without interference in their religious beliefs and practices.

But as Afonso sailed around expanding his base and spice trade, the Jesuits fanned out spreading their avowed faith. Establishing the first chapel of St. Catherine in the capital Goa city, they went about proselytizing, building chapels and crosses, at times of mud and thatched roofs, in the nearby Bardez and Ilhas *talukas*.

The Inquisition established in Portugal in 1536, was brought to Goa by 1560. It was at its peak during the dynastic Iberian union of Portugal and Spain (1580-1640). Through the period, the viceroys and governors began implementing what was decreed by the kings and approved by the seal of the *papal bull*, completing most of the churches in the *Old Conquests*, hounding the heathens and vandalizing anything the Inquisitor branded as a vestige of paganism.

CHAPTER I

The OVK Triad

The three southern villages of Osnem, Velem and Kunkali skirted by river Sal were the last bastion of resistance the Portuguese encountered on their march to convert the local population 4-5 decades after the capture of Goa.

Four centuries on, this OVK village triad was now home to the 20th generation of the converts' descendants who rarely ventured out, be it for marriages or socializing.

To the east, Osnem and Kunkali were joined by a high bund road that bisected an expanse of low-lying paddy fields. Every monsoon torrent would turn one side of the bund into a seasonal lake, flooding the other side too.

Eons before the arrival of the dynasties or the Portuguese, the whole low valley was a perennial lake, a habitat for fish, otter and the crocodile. The settlers had yet to arrive and villages yet to be named. As they arrived they built bunds, culverts and canals converting the low valleys into crop fields. They settled on the adjacent garden lands and named their villages. Then they parceled out the fields to themselves for ownership and collective farming.

Bandar village, a ward of Osnem, had six bunds connecting to its six sub-wards. As other villages had the same or similar name, it probably originated from the word *bund* or *bandh*.

CHAPTER II

Mates by Fate

It was the summer of 1951. Fifteen year old Bruno had come to collect his report at the English school he had joined a year ago having done Class III of Portuguese school; it was the first English school that had come up in Osnem village in mid 1930s.

Bruno was among the top rankers. Standing in the narrow school yard with his report in hand, he looked in front at the towering statue of Christ the King and then ahead at the church cross that lay shrouded by a red bloom of *gulmohar*. He made a sign of the cross and opened the report. As he scanned his mark-sheet he felt a breath down his neck, his nostrils drawing in an acrid whiff.

"You've done well, you stood second."
Bruno turned round and saw a tall gangly boy.

"What's your name? You aren't from this school. But I've seen you playing football for a youth club."

"I am Caetano Silva from Velem. But boys know me as Caitu. Call me whatever you like. I've just joined this school. A boy up in the verandah pointed you out as my classmate this year. He said you are from Bandar and a good student and a footballer too. I am looking for a good friend; quite often I end up in the wrong company."

He spoke briskly.

"Nice to meet you; where were you earlier?" asked Bruno

"I was three years in the seminary and then two years in a boarding school. That was until last year when I decided not to go back there."

"So you lost a year. What's the reason?" asked Bruno

"The reason….reason… *he paused*….the reason…… my sister…she didn't want me to go away from home," he mumbled

"Your elder sister, did she hold you back?" quizzed Bruno

"No, my little sister kept me back."

"What happened?"

"Last summer I came home on vacation. A week before I was to leave for my boarding school, my sister developed a sore throat. Our family physician told us she is having sore tonsils. But she didn't improve with his medicine. On the third day her jaw swelled and the physician said she is having mumps. *'There is an epidemic, but it's not a serious illness. She will be fine by weekend.' he said.* My sister was nine, a lively playful child. She kept up her spirits. In a couple of days her lump eased but her spirits were down. She became lethargic but said she is feeling fine.

'I don't understand why her pulse is so low,' muttered the physician.

'So, should we get another doctor to consult?' asked my *mama.* He agreed for a joint consultation." Caitu paused and resumed:

"We brought in a Bombay doctor who was on vacation. After a feedback from our physician, he checked my sister's pulse, her temperature and then with his torch he looked deep down into her throat. In an instant his face turned grave.

He stared at our physician and exchanged a few words with him. Then he said to my mama: *'Take the girl to the hospital right now.'*

Caitu paused swallowing a lump in his throat.

"And then?" asked Bruno.

"My sister died in the hospital the next day of diphtheria." Caitu tried to choke an emotion that ended a sniffle.

Bruno looked down for a while.

"My deepest sympathies, Caitu. What was her name?"

"Ann Marie."

"My mother's name is Ana," said Bruno

"It's been a year and I am quite over it now. It hurts for a while. My sister was like one night's sweet dream that lingers like real through the long night and suddenly you wake up empty. It doesn't hurt me anymore. I am fine now and more carefree than before. I feel the spirit of my sister is in me now," said Caitu spluttering a girlish giggle and added:

"Bruno! Well, that's your name I'm told. I've just heard they're showing a movie at your church this evening, a movie in color for the first time."

"Our chaplain spoke of it this morning. I had seen my first movie with my father years ago. As a kid, I was thrilled to see lifelike images moving on the church wall. My father stopped seeing these films; he says these are Portuguese propaganda films of their conquests.

He watches Hindi movies in Bombay. As he is around I cannot stay out late in the evenings. I might come if I get some company from the village," Bruno responded

"Where is your bicycle?"

"I don't have one. But I enjoy the morning walk to school, especially after attending the early service at our chapel. I am a regular altar boy there."

"Well, I could fetch you from home on my bicycle or you meet me in the bazaar at six. I will reach you home after the show. My bicycle has a powerful dynamo. The lamp is like a searchlight," said Caitu pointing to the bicycle parked by a mango tree

Bruno thought for a while: "Alright, in the bazaar at six is fine."

"I shall see you then." Instantly someone gave a shout: "Oi Caitu" Two boys wearing identical gaudy apparel stood on the road.

"Look Bruno, these are boogie-woogie twins. They are cousins and good dancers. In their childhood we knew them as Ronaldo and Bonifacio. Then they went to Bombay and studied in an English school. Now they are back and call themselves Ronnie & Bonnie." Caitu waved out to the boys and hurried down to meet them.

CHAPTER III

The Movie at the Church

A feature of the rural wards was the alternative routes that bypassed the main road. Walking the crisscrossing sand paths Bruno reached the bazaar, a square of row-shops with tiled roofs: a grocery-cum-stationary shop, a pharmacy, a post-office, a café, a tailor shop and cycle-for-rent were the prominent ones; a fish-market under a shed stood apart. While the *taberna* serving imported liquor also had a prominent spot, the local *feni* pub stood at a wayside nook.

It was about seven when Caitu rode in, late by an hour. He gave Bruno a wayward excuse and cycled off with him to the churchyard.

The church façade with its triangular gable with a crucifix at the apex and an oculus at its base stood perpendicular to a large side wall behind which were the priest's residence and the offices of the parish and the *Comunidade.* The whitewashed wall had served as a movie screen ever since the film shows had begun. That evening a new screen was put up. Right behind, at a table cluttered with spools and boxes, sat a Portuguese soldier; beside him on a tripod, a projector buzzed.

A hundred odd villagers had assembled to watch. Squatted on the ground below the screen were the kids, girls and boys, and behind them in the first row of seats were special invitees: the priests, Prof. Leitão, the *regidor* and the village elders. The three hind rows were a gender mix with fewer women. Behind them were the standees, a throng of boys and men.

Caitu pulled Bruno aside to sit with him at the threshold of the church front door, not far from the restive kids near the screen.

The color of images flashing on the screen stood out despite the twilight: two little jumpy creatures zig-zagged amid whistles, crashes, screeches and whooshes, syncopated by orchestral music. Their unending battles seemed to delight the kids and the elders alike. It was a Tom & Jerry cartoon show.

As the night grew the picture became sharper and finer.

But the change of reel brought forth a documentary in Black & White disappointing the kids:

It opened with two stills of sailing ships: a caravel with two triangular sails and a n*au*, a large cargo ship with square and triangular sails. Then, in the backdrop of the Belém Tower by the River Tagus, a flotilla of ships sailed out of the Lisbon port. As they sailed off, a close-up shot on a *nau* focused on a bearded man in a black circular cap. A Portuguese voiceover that only a few understood tried to rise above the drone of the projector. A boy seated in the front turned round:

"Professor, is the bearded man Vasco da Gama or Afonso de Albuquerque? But they were dead long time ago," he uttered

"He is Vasco da Gama, the great explorer setting out on São Gabriel on his first voyage to India. This is a recreation of the historic scene. Now stop disturbing when the movie is on," the professor shouted back

"Got it," mumbled the boy

Spanning across scenes of picturesque islands and tranquil blue seas, another close-up showed a navigator on a deck looking at his compass and then at the sea chart. Beside him a longhaired bearded man in majestic uniform gazed at a distant murky coast.

"Caitu, he is Afonso de Albuquerque," Bruno whispered; he had his eye and the ear tuned in.

"He is peering into the dark horizon, not knowing he is passing by Madeira or the African coast," Caitu blurted out sniggering, as professor darted a sharp glance towards the boys. Then a swift transition played out a sequence of gripping scenes:

An entire fleet is caught in a severe storm; as winds and high waves batter the boats tossing them up and down and rolling them side to side, sailors cling to the masts to stay afloat. Of a sudden, the high waves morph into monsters swallowing up a number of ships. A little boy in the front turns round:

"Are the monsters real Father?" he asks the priest

"Of course, there are sea monsters in the deep ocean; that's how half the boats and men did not find their way back to Lisboa. Now, be quiet and watch." It was the professor who cut in again.

The change of reel saw the color in motion shift to Africa: as half-clad tribal men did a mock war dance, their women jiggled to the furious ethnic drum beats arousing the curiosity of both the kids and the elders. Duels of sword-fights and spear-fights by horse riders set off a loud chatter among the squatted children. They were quieted down by rebukes from behind.

Then, a round-up of scenes from around Portugal evoked a buzz among the viewers. It was like a home-coming. From church congregations, feasts and processions, to gala fairs and brass bands, to revelers in theatrical masks at a street carnival -the scenes had long been a part of their own ritual. The festive montage ended with couples in graceful attire doing the *corridinho,* the run-and-rotate Portuguese folk dance, to the strains of accordions.

An avenue bustling with classic and vintage cars, a sidewalk with urbane commuters in a rush and a street of yellow tram cars- the snapshots capsulized the Lisbon of the 1950s. The scene shifted to the museum district of Belém.

Taking a long and mid shot of an imposing sprawling monastery with an ornate tower and steeples tipped with crosses, the camera zoomed into its interior onto a decorated casket.

Following the voiceover, Bruno gave a feedback to Caitu:

"Inside that casket lie the remains of Vasco da Gama, who died in India on his second visit. This is the Jerónimos Monastery. It is also the resting place of the few kings of Aviz and Braganza dynasties, not forgetting the great poet Luis de Camões who wrote during his stay in Goa; but he was in a prison."

Caitu nudged Bruno as select scenes of the monastery's vast interior played out on the screen.

"My uncle told me Vasco da Gama was also a pirate. He looted unarmed Arab boats and if an Indian ruler turned him away he fired canons towards their shore. Afonso de Albuquerque was even worse; he maimed or hanged his own soldiers if they deserted. But he has a special place here and lies buried as per his wish in the chapel of Madonna of the Mount; I had been there." Caitu cut short as Bruno elbowed him.

"Stop your extra commentary. Professor is watching us. The soldiers are here. Don't make trouble for us," the boy grumbled

Spanning across forts and museums, spotlighting the solemn portraits of dukes, kings and emperors hung on walls, the film ended with a *fadista* in a white gown singing a soulful *fado* on the Tower of Belém.

The screen blanked out as the soldier bellowed for attention. The dignitaries in the first row stood up.

"Everybody stand up please," shouted the professor as the national flag fluttered on the screen to a chorus of *'A Portuguesa'*. He lent it a tenor.

As the anthem ended, Caitu and Bruno got up to leave.

"I never understood the lines fully even though I had to sing the anthem at the seminary so often. Did you Bruno?" asked Caitu

"It's a solemn tribute to her heroes by a small but great seafaring nation: *Heroes of the sea, noble people/ Brave immortal nation, raise today again the splendor of Portugal.*"

"Stop parroting your professor, Bruno. The splendor of Portugal has long faded away," Caitu taunted

As the crowd dispersed Bruno and Caitu decided to go away. But Caitu seemed agitated at the sight of Ronnie and Bonnie standing behind the churchyard balustrade.

"Hold on a minute boy; that rascal Bonnie needs a bashing. He's spreading tales about my cousin Filu, saying she's a flirt only because she refused to dance with him." He charged towards the duo he had shown great delight to meet the previous day. Instantly, Bruno heard a familiar voice:

"Brúnu, Brúnu!"

It was the professor, Bruno's Portuguese teacher and principal of the school he had attended until Class Three when he switched to English school. As Bruno turned round, the professor stopped to speak to a soldier who was packing up the equipment.

Professor was quite upset by Bruno's move. When Bruno had gone with his father to see him regarding the Leaving Certificate, Leitão had given his father an earful. The two were childhood companions and had played football together. Professor was seated in a tall arm chair with his coat hanging behind.

'Good morning Prof. Leitão, it gives me great pleasure to see you in the Principal's chair, with your coat hung behind it' Roque had exclaimed.

'Good morning Roque, I wish you had allowed your son to complete his high school in Portuguese. He was a ranker and would have finished with distinction. I recall you did a few classes of English school and now you're scrubbing the ship deck. Perhaps you want to make him a butler. I am quite upset. Do you want him to relive your experience, a life of stormy seas and loneliness away from home?' Leitão had snapped back

"Bruno, come aside please," uttered Leitão, interrupting the boy's musing. Darting a scornful glance at the boys who had got into a heated argument, he blurted out:

"I had cautioned your father not to leave our school. My advice wasn't heeded. And now you've found this rowdy buddy. Are you aware that he is under the watch of *Polícia Secreta*? His uncle Stalin, an enemy of the State is a communist like his mentor, the doctor who only writes pamphlets on socialism that he calls freedom." He glared at Caitu who had now caught Bonnie's arm. He resumed in a sterner tone:

"Bruno, be careful! The police now have extraordinary powers. If any Indian citizen working against the state gets caught, they will thrash and hurl him over the border. But they will not spare your companion or you, the Portuguese citizens. You will be jailed here or shipped to Portugal. You're young and vulnerable. Try to keep away from this boy, Cai Cait...."

"Caetano, professor," said Bruno as they heard a vocal outburst

"Look! He is hitting the boy." Rushing closer to the action, the professor yelled: "Hoi, you loafers, stop fighting; the *regidor* and the police are here. I will have you arrested."

As Caitu cut short his assault, Leitão retraced his steps.

"Bruno, please be careful! I am going now. I can drop you home," he said

"Thank you professor; I have to buy a few things in the bazaar." The slim erect man hurried towards the Beetle parked nearby.

The three walked towards Bruno as if nothing had happened.

"Looks like you guys have settled; why did you hit him Caitu?"

"Hear me Bruno. Bonnie first denied Filu's allegation. But what he said next made me really angry. He said people talk about me and my uncle, that we are communists and anti-church." Bonnie was quick to rebut:

"Caitu, I said it just to let you know what Filu said about me and what I heard about you are only rumors."

"Alright, let the matter rest now. I shall get back after a full enquiry; sorry for the punches. I am quite worked up these days. I have even stopped going to church. That doesn't mean I am a communist."

He shook hands with the boys and they cycled off. He turned to Bruno:

"Sorry for the distraction. I tend to get worked up. Let's walk for a while."

"Bonnie seems to be a decent chap. You're picking up fights for nothing. Well, tell me, you really stopped going to church? No wonder you ran away from the seminary. May be your parents sent you there against your wish."

"No, it was me who was adamant at first. As a child, I was struck by the grandeur of the church, on the outside and within: its façade, the belfry, the ornate altars and the images. The priestly vestments, the oratory and the respect the priest commanded from the worshippers fascinated me. My dedication to church service made the vicar predict that I would be a priest one day. I pestered my parents until they gave in to my wish. At the seminary, I was ecstatic at first. But two years on, I just couldn't stick to the routine and the discipline.

Moreover, my sister was growing smart, talkative and playful. My annual visits made me grow fonder of her.

I started complaining to the Superior and the Rector of headaches and told them I wish to quit. Then I told my parents I don't want to be a priest. And on my third summer visit I refused to go back. My folks though surprised finally gave in. My father then forced me either to go to Belgaum or join a boarding school in Goa. I opted for a boarding school three ferries away. You know the rest of the story." Caitu rambled on and ended with a query as they made it to the bazaar: " Should I take you home now?"

"You go straight home. I have to buy milk and cheese. I would go with my father if he is around."

"When is your father leaving?"

"Just this afternoon he got a postcard to report for medical. He has to do his medical before joining the ship. He should be going next week," said Bruno

The bazaar was a picture of near darkness except the two main groceries that dazzled under Petromax lamps; the tea shop and the *taberna* were lit by chimney lamps. A few vehicles were parked in the center of the square. Bruno looked around for his father and was told that he had already left.

"How long will you take to do your purchase Bruno?" asked Caitu

"Five minutes perhaps, but there's bit of a crowd there. Its closing time you know."

"Never mind, take your time. I have to pass on an urgent message. I will be back in a few minutes," he retorted

"Thank you Caitu. You go straight home. I shall walk my way home."

"No, you wait for me," he shouted and cycled the way they had come

It took longer than expected to do the purchase. Then as Bruno turned round to leave, he saw Caitu waiting in the shadows.

"I told you I will manage. You know our villages are safe to walk around any time of the day or night except for dogs or a random snake that might come your way. But I have a torch here," he said touching his pocket

"No way, Bruno; I will reach you up to your chapel and then you may walk. I will be back here in ten minutes. I could also cut through from the back of your village dropping you closer to home. I am familiar with the area from there on. With this new Raleigh bicycle with a powerful lamp, I could go anywhere anytime."

At last, Bruno agreed for a drop up to the chapel. Caitu pedaled away with renewed gusto, crooning a song. Seated on the front tube, whiffy vapors attacked Bruno's nostrils. Despite his crooning Caitu's hands were firm on the handle bars. When they reached the chapel Bruno asked him to hold on:

"What's this Caitu? You had a drink somewhere in five minutes. You can't hide it? You smell of it strong; at this age, you are only sixteen?"

"I am seventeen, lost a year after my sister died as I stayed at home."

"I heard that you are a fine footballer. But please don't drink liquor. Tea is fine. Good night," said Bruno and started walking

"I don't do it regularly. I was quite excited about you accepting my companionship. You know most boys don't want to be too friendly with me. Alright, you meet me in the bazaar tomorrow for a cup of tea at four in the afternoon. We will go down the river and have a chat. Good night," Caitu burst into his girlish giggle as he rode off

CHAPTER IV

A chat by the side stream

The next day afternoon the boys met in the bazaar and had tea. With Bruno sitting on the front bar, Caitu cycled towards the riverside. Parking the bicycle by the church boundary wall, he suggested that they sit by the bank. They sat there with their legs dangling over the murky water flowing upstream. Away to their right two old men were seated on a stone bench. Further up was the ferry with a slide landing for country boats. Caitu began in haste:

"We have a football game tomorrow. You can join us. It's a friendly match but there's prize money of hundred rupias offered by a well-wisher. Besides, you'll get patties and soft drinks after the match."

"I am not that big Caitu and can't match your pace. You all must be big boys. Moreover, I must return home by seven. Mother's timetable when father is around."

"No problem. We start at five and finish by six. I'll reach you home in time. We're all a mixed bunch, young and old. There's neither age limit nor limit to number of players. In summer as we have many players, we field a team of up to 15 players or more to a side. In the rains we have fewer players as boys go back after their vacation; and also fewer playgrounds as the fields get waterlogged. Would you come?"

"Caitu, I have to take father's permission. He would ask me, where, when and who invited you?" Caitu butted in before Bruno could finish:

"And if you say, Caetano, a nephew of Santolino alias Stalin, he might not like it."

"My father won't complain against playing football, any place it might be. He also supports freedom movement but not violence. He is a peaceful man though he smokes fifteen cigarettes and 6-8 cups of tea daily."

"Not good man. My grandma died smoking her own cheroot cones. Anyway, I will wait till your father leaves. We still have a month and a half of holidays left. Next Sunday I am inviting you for lunch. I will pick you up from the chapel after the service.

If you like we could go fishing at the Xapo lake. It is already harvested but has loads of fish still. I will teach you a few things, like swimming, diving, rowing the boat and climbing a coconut tree; and also teach you to play banjo and sing."

"Oh you have so many talents, but I won't climb a coconut tree to steal someone's coconuts; my father smacked me once for attempting it," grumbled Bruno

"Boys aren't supposed to go to church and school only. They must have fun too; like playing football, swimming or go boating on the river or lake. And you can't call them thieves if they pluck a few tender coconuts or poach some fish. It's a part of growing up. We do it for a while and pass over that phase. And don't you tell me your father hasn't done anything of the sort? My father did it but never talked to me about it; may be because he is a big butler now." Caitu paused. The two men got up from the bench and walked away.

As eagles circled above the river a long narrow boat came in filled with a ragtag of bundles, cycles and a few people. The road from the bazaar had ended by the river, and resumed on the opposite bank which was a flood-prone expanse of fish ponds and salt pans lying between two streams of river Sal. It cut into that expanse and wended its way through a string of villages to reach the district town.

"I can see a *carreira* on the other side of the bank," said Bruno

"They call it *caminhão* in the north. Both the seminary and then the boarding school I went to were in the north. It would take me three river ferries and four *caminhãos* to get there. The point is....."

"Anyway the words mean the same thing: *caminhão,* a lorry, *carreira,* the route. I am proud of this local ingenuity: a tin-body mounted on the Dodge or Chevrolet chassis, converting into a 20-plus-seater minibus. They do it in Kunkali," he paused, "but what was the point? Sorry, I cut you off there."

"The point is my father felt staying far from home would keep me away from bad company. But then you know what happened next," mumbled Caitu

This time a bigger boat overloaded with a larger load rode in. It had men, women and children and cyclists and it swayed unsteadily. As it neared the bank the craft lurched sideways missing the landing. The boatman vaulted on the pole to the bank and swiftly pulled the boat to anchorage.

"That boatman made a mistake but corrected himself in time. I have been on a boat ride with Stalin. He is an ace," said Caitu

"I don't know why they don't have a proper ferry here. These narrow canoes of tree trunks wobble or sink low into the water. Though the river isn't very wide, it's a big risk for children and women," grumbled Bruno

"Ah ha, Bruno! You may ask your professor, the Salazar supporter. For the past four centuries Portuguese have only built culverts over streams and rivulets. Tell me, what was he telling you last evening? What was he shouting about? It was just a boys' scuffle. I think he is keeping an eye on me. He knows I am Stalin's nephew. I used to think many called my uncle a communist because of his name. But once I went through a book he had left at home. It was called The Communist Manifesto.

By the way, he has just arrived from Bombay. Have you heard of Goa Freedom Party? Stalin says they are the real freedom fighters. Fed up with the peaceful approach they began a bombing campaign a few years ago that shook the Portuguese." Bruno was quick to respond:

"Well, professor spoke of GFP once. He said they were a mere flash in the pan and that their bombs had killed their own and a few innocent men. He said then they fled across the border and were not heard of. But Caitu, let the seniors bother about freedom. Let's finish our school first. We're lucky to have the first English school in our village. I have set my eyes on Africa. A relative has offered to help."

"Good for you. I don't know where I will go and what I will do. May be I will go to Bombay. Every João or Pedro from here head to that city and find something or hop on the ship where beer is just a few cents. So why not Caitu give it a try?" he sniggered

"That's shameful. Your father is a butler. You have enough money to study and come up in life. I can help you with your studies, especially with math, science or Portuguese. But for now, I can meet you only after my father leaves," Bruno asserted

They've been sitting there for over an hour. The shadows from the banks stretched over the river that snaked eastward on the upstream. To their left, the surface waters showed a gloomy reflection of the church side and the extended edifice that stood at the very edge of the river. Caitu got up abruptly.

"I will reach you home," he said and walked to his bicycle

"Not today, I will walk home with my father. He will be around at the tea shop chatting with someone," said Bruno

"Before I forget, Stalin has arranged for a boat ride right up to the lighthouse. His friend owns boats and has an ancestral cottage in the forest by the sea. Stalin sometimes goes there with his colleagues. This time he wants to take school boys. Tell me if you're interested. It will be fun out in the sea," Caitu enthused

"I will see about that. Now, you said your uncle had a book on Communism. He must be a communist then. Did he try to influence you?" asked Bruno as he hopped on the front bar

"People say that of Stalin. He has put a few ideas in my head here and there, like collective ownership of property or a classless society. He says people are ignorant about the true essence of communism and take it as anti-church. He says in a sense Christ was a true socialist. But both at the church and at the seminary, I was taught that Communism is anti-church. Does your father speak to you on this matter?"

"He once spoke of Vladivostok or Odessa, ports in the communist USSR where they have women guards as big and strong as their men. They maintain a stony silence and only give directions by hand. My father says the government is communist but people outside the port though poor are friendly and seem very religious."

Before they parted Bruno told Caitu that he would meet him in the bazaar next Sunday at 11, but only if his father had left.

CHAPTER V

For Lunch at Caetano's

A seafarer's home has a disruptive family life pattern; father's joyful homecoming and then a goodbye a few months on is traumatic for an oversensitive growing child, more so for a boy than a girl though most adults get acclimatized after a while. Bruno soon outgrew that trauma as he spent more time outdoors playing or interacting with his peers. A parting hug from his father did make him tearful followed by an emptiness for a few days. But he was in his teens now and had seen his grandparents go. Beneath the layer of sadness of parting lay a streak of mild comfort, as his ever-watchful father handed over the charge of his supervision to his easy-going mother.

But Bruno knew in his heart that he would not exceed certain boundaries he had set for himself. Though he studied well and still served regularly at the chapel, mother noticed that of late he had begun to take a few liberties on some pretext. She didn't resent it so long as he didn't do it often. Days before his father's arrival she had cautioned him when he had come an hour late.

"I don't like this late home-coming Bruno; lest your father point a finger at me and accuse me: 'look, how wayward he has become under your supervision," she had said

Though he knew that his son had grown into a responsible boy, Roque had his inner fears of what might happen when he wasn't at home. It was his habit to have a one to one conversation with his son before he left for his voyage. That evening it was the *balcão* talk.

"Bruno, I know you're much more intelligent and sensible than me or your mother. So I need not lecture you on how you should conduct yourself. I trust you and have great expectations of you. Please don't let me down. Don't you do anything unbecoming of you; don't associate with boys with dubious character."

The same night as they lay in bed, Roque and Ana kept chatting well past midnight. While he advised her to make do with his limited earnings and get a better crop yield, Ana grumbled on with a litany of her complaints. But his final remark put her on her guard: " I know Bruno is vulnerable as I was at his age. I want him to pass his matric with distinction. You know there are excellent schools in Belgaum. But you always tell me he is doing fine here and that you are in control of things. But there are things beyond your control."

As Roque fell off to sleep, Ana remained awake pondering over. She knew his cousin sister lived in Belgaum and that Roque did things on the quiet. And knowing that Roque and Leitão were childhood companions, she suspected Leitão was keeping an eye on Bruno and keeping her husband posted.

Days later Bruno's father left home to join the ship at the end of a two-month vacation.

A day before Sunday Bruno told mother that he is invited for lunch by a new friend from Velem.

"Lunching with a new friend? How come you are invited soon after your father left? Your father seemed worried in the last few days. He has asked me to keep an eye on you. He must have heard something. Who is this new friend?" asked Ana, seemingly annoyed

"The boy is my new classmate. He is tall and strong, a good football player. He can do anything; fish, swim, climb coconut trees and what not. What's wrong with going for lunch? Don't worry mãe, he comes from a good family. His father is a butler."

"Oh, how quickly you knew about his family? And he climbs coconut trees! Stealing coconuts?" she protested

"What I meant was he is good at many things mãe. He also knows to sing and play banjo."

"But take care Bruno; your father keeps telling me that you are at a susceptible age just like he was," she moaned

Simpering, Bruno walked up to her and gave a peck on the cheek. A faint smile lit up her face.

"I will let you go this time. But before you do anything more with this boy I want to see him and want to know about his family."

"Surely mãe," said Bruno touching her head. "Let me go for a game now," he added

The next day Caitu picked Bruno at Osnem bazaar and turned southwards to Velem. On the way as they passed by a large mansion, Caitu remarked:

"I heard the mansion belongs to the descendants of a Khan or a Shah who converted. Is it true?"

"I don't know and am not interested to know?" snapped Bruno

Turning left behind the Velem church, Caitu cycled across its front and stopped a little ahead by the cemetery wall.

"Bruno, this might please you. They say it took nearly 200 years to build this church after you church."

"I know, earlier you had a chapel. It was filial to our church but what's your point?" asked Bruno

"My point is that our church has a proper façade. Look at its belfry right in the center, unlike your church. The best thing I like about the church or chapel is their bell towers. I once went right up there and tolled the bell. I love the deafening resonance. Your chapel also has a similar belfry, but not your church; to me, it looks more like a monastery. But you and I have heard a few things." Caitu cut short seeing a priest walk out from his residence.

"Let's move now. The vicar wanted to see me. I haven't been to church for a month now. He thinks I have become a communist like Stalin. Actually nothing of the sort; I just hate waking up early in the morning."

Caitu rode off towards his village. Pedaling hard over a sandy pathway he got on a harder mud road winding between houses on either side. A sandy open patch led to the house. It was the last house and behind it a narrow bund joined a high embankment below which lay a large low-lying field.

"Bruno, below that high embankment is the Xapo lake, and to the right are the hills," said Caitu pointing out to it

Keeping the bicycle aside, he led Bruno up a flight of steps. An identical flight of steps came up from other side that had a garden. There were flower pots alongside the steps. In the balcony they were met with two ladies seated on the two front seats.

"Bruno, this is my mama and that's my cousin Filomena; Filu is her pet name," he turned round,

"Mama, Bruno, my new classmate I had spoken to you of; he is from Bandar ward of Osnem. Very studious and calm lad, unlike me," he sniggered

Mama got up and hugged Bruno as if she had known him, while Filu gave a peck on the cheek. The boys sat on the cement bench facing the front door.

"Caetano always talks about you. I am glad that he finally found a friend like you Bruno. May God bless you always," said mama and pried Bruno with a few personal queries, with Filu jumping in between: *"do you have any relatives in Velem? ...oh a cousin at Baga?... what's his sister's or mother's name?"*

"Enough mama, please get a soft drink for him; we would be in the sitting room," said Caitu and turned round, "let's go in Bruno."

"I will get it for him just now," said mama and walked in with Filu in tow

Caitu led Bruno in, turning right into a large well-furnished room. Walking behind Bruno noticed a large glass showcase and a gramophone by the two windows overlooking the garden. At the rear wall h u n g a c l o c k , a book shelf with a desk to one side and a double-ledged narrow cabinet by a small door that lay shut. Spaced around the center was a pair of settees face-to-face, flanked by arm chairs and single chairs with cushions atop the cane seats. On a star design in the middle of the cemented floor was a circular table. Hung on the walls, were B & W framed photos.
 Caitu's mama came in with the drink. She put the glass on the table: "Have it Bruno, its raspberry," she said
"Oh raspberry, nice, thank you auntie," replied Bruno

As his mama exited the room, Caitu showed Bruno around. He started with an account of the photos:

"That's my grandpa with a twirling moustache with grandma; and there, my parents on their wedding day. Look here at the foursome: my papa, mama holding the baby girl and the school boy, that's me.... Those books in the shelf belong to Alberto. And over there, that's the oval mirror between the windows."

Bruno cut in: "Caetano, don't waste your breath

describing the furniture? Tell me about the two photos on either side of the mirror."

"You're right Bruno. To the left is my step mother who is no more and to the right is her son Alberto, my step brother." Then he led Bruno back to the gramophone. It was placed on a table with a chest of drawers on one side. He pulled open a drawer.

"Have a look Bruno at the collection. Though papa had kept everything tagged and labeled it tends to get messed up." He thumbed through a stack of records. There were labels like Victor, Decca, RCA and HMV.

He shut the drawer back and opened another below it. There were more stacks with hand written notes batching the genre of music: dance music, big band, quartets, bolero, rumba & samba or waltz and songs from the charts.

"There are few more in the bottom drawer; those are Portuguese, Hindi and records of Goan singers."

"And how long these records play? We had at home that played for 3 minutes," said Bruno

"There are also 10 & 12 inch records that play for 3-6 six minutes," replied Caitu

"Surely, your papa must have spent a fortune," exclaimed Bruno

"He had a craze for records. When he came home this box would play for hours on end. It's less now. I broke the old phonograph with the golden horn, crashing the pedestal along with it. Though I was a kid I was spanked. It was my grandpa's," he uttered chuckling

He asked Bruno to have the drink and survey around like his own home, and walked out of the room.

Bruno walked around sipping his drink. He became curious of the double-ledged cabinet. It was glass-fronted to one side, displaying colorful bottles of concentrates; its other door was brown hardwood with separate keyhole. He had seen such cabinets that separated wines and syrups in some houses.

Bruno walked back to the two layered glass show case. In the upper section he saw two framed photos of a little girl. In one she had worn a black blouse over a red tulle skirt; in the other she was standing in a white-lace gown holding a candle and a flower bouquet in her hands. The photos were slanted to make space for a jumble of dolls and trinkets. In the lower section amidst a clutter of sports mementos like cups and medals, lying flat was a banjo. As Bruno leaned to look closely at the photos, he felt someone was standing behind him.

"Oh Caitu, tell me about this photo." Turning round he saw his mama instead.

"That's my Ann Marie. Her papa used to make her dance wearing that red skirt. Caetano has filled in all her toys there. That banjo there, he has not played since she left." She heaved a deep sigh: "It was not just a mistake but total carelessness. That's what the consulting doctor confessed to us. Caetano is totally broken. He's not showing it. How many brothers and sisters do you have?"

"None, I wish I had one sister," said Bruno.

She glanced at the photo and sighed.

She left as Caitu came in and plumped on the settee pulling Bruno to sit there. They chatted for a few minutes.

"Alright, I will spin a disk that Ann often danced to," he said and shuffled to the gramophone. He picked a disc and put it on the turntable. As the needle hit the groove it pumped out a fast paced music, a blend of accordions and symphony.

Caitu came back and sat with Bruno. "What kind of music is it? It's too furious a pace for a kid Caetano," said Bruno as Caitu mused aloud:

"Papa often played this record just to watch Ann dance wearing a red tulle skirt. You can see that photo there. It's also called can-can music; papa said he had watched the dancers at Monte Carlo.

But Ann danced like a kid, back and forth hopping or circling. Then papa would play our folk songs, the records of Konkani *dekhni* or *mando* and opera songs recorded in France by our earliest artists. He would sing along as she jigged until she dropped down exhausted. Then he would pick her up and dance to this song." Before Caitu could play it, Filu called them for lunch.

The dining table was laid out with bowls of rice, chicken *xacuti*, prawn curry, spinach and fillets of king fish fried. For the dessert there were mangoes and bananas.

A minute after the boys had sat down Filu joined at the table. As mama kept pushing dishes towards Bruno coaxing him to have more of this or that, Caitu spoke to Filu of the Bonnie incident and it turned into an argument.

"And why did you hit him Caitu? I've now come to know it was someone else who made the story about Bonnie. He was after me too," Filu whined

"You are a spoiler Filu. Why didn't you find out first? Now I am a bad boy. I've never had problems with Bonnie and Ronnie," he snapped at her

"Say I am sorry. I would when I meet him. No need to feel sour about it. We will catch hold of that boy next," she exhorted

"Filu, you're like a flirting wind that sings broken tunes. Don't come to me again with your complaints," Caitu yelled back while mama tried to calm him down. As Bruno ate quietly with his head down, Filu got up and walked away with her plate.

After lunch Caitu ushered Bruno him into their sitting room asking him to rest for a while.

"Play that song your papa danced picking Ann up. Play it please," said the boy

Caitu played it and when it ended Bruno exclaimed:

"Beautiful tune and lyrics Caetano; I would love to have one though my gramophone is broken down. Isn't it titled Ramona? I heard it on BBC and Radio Jakarta."

"It is Ramona by Gene Austin. Here's another by the same singer, My Blue Heaven."

As Caitu kept changing records, Bruno began to doze on the settee. Caitu stopped the music and told Bruno to lie down; then he lay down on other settee.

Later his mama announced it was tea time. She served pancakes with coconut and *jaggery* filling to go with a mug of weak red tea. Then Caitu had a suggestion.

"Let's join the boys for a game in the fields. And then I will reach you home from there."

"I am a bit tired Caetano. You go down and play while I sit and watch,"

"Oh! You've been calling me by my real name. I think you are worried what my mother would think. Don't you worry? She knows everybody calls me Caitu."

"Certainly, I don't like these nicknames. They're often invented by boys to mock you. But yours is fine. Some senior boys who had been in Bombay used to call me *Brun pão*, the crusty bread they bake there."

"I said I don't mind my nick name but I won't call you that," Caitu chuckled

Moments later, when they were about to leave, a man of moderate build came cycling; leaning his bicycle by the wall, he came up the steps.

"Where are you off to Caitu, and who's this kid here?" he asked

"He is Bruno, my new classmate from Bandar. He is diligent and well-mannered. His father is a Gandhi follower." As Bruno made a face, Caitu turned round: "Bruno, this is my uncle Stalin I spoke to you of." Bruno gave him a polite nod.

"Good for you Caitu! Bandar men are good fighters. By the way, we are going on a picnic tomorrow, me and my colleague.

You get him and a few more boys whose fathers don't brag about the Portuguese. We will meet a teacher of history. I am sure it will be fun and a learning experience for you boys," said Stalin

"Where are we going Stalin?" asked Caitu

"To the cave; haven't you been there before? It will be an hour's brisk walk by the foothill. We will take water and some sandwiches."

"But what sandwiches? Can we eat meat sandwiches there? That's the Pandava cave, isn't it?"

Stalin chuckled: "That's just a belief. I had once seen a calf carcass in the cave. A leopard could have had its meal there. I will speak to Marta about the sandwiches. Fish cutlets or even boiled eggs will do. We should leave by 8:30. You go ahead but don't play for long. You will be tired," he said and walked inside

CHAPTER VI

Picnic at the Pandava Cave

The next morning, Bruno rented a bicycle and reached Caitu's house. Stalin was seated in the balcony with a man Bruno had heard of.

"You're son of Roque from Bandar, isn't it?" he asked as Bruno came up

"Yes I am, Marcus," said Bruno

"Well, you know me by name though I am not from your village," retorted Marcus

"Of course, everybody knows you guys around the three villages as you are working for some cause. I have seen you with my father sometimes."

"I know your father because he is a patriot. We chat over a cup of tea whenever we meet in your bazaar. But did you say we're working for some cause? We are working to free you of the yoke round your neck. Good that you've come. You must know some history and geography of our three villages." Marcus turned to Stalin.

"Are we set to go?"

"Almost; Caitu is packing up sandwiches. It's quite warm and humid you know. But the breeze across the hill will refresh us as we walk," said Stalin

Setting out, as they passed by the Xapo lake, Marcus remarked:

"Boys, have a look! This is a low lying field that turns into a lake and stays so for months during the rains.

A canal comes winding from the 'Twelve Bunds' of Kunkali, where they have built check-dams to conserve water for irrigation. But in the rains, they release water in all directions flooding our fields like this one here. It might give you some fish but we can't grow our paddy or vegetables. But right now this is neither a field nor a lake but a barren swamp. It's the same story after four centuries of Portuguese rule; no dams, no canals to grow three crops in a year." Bruno butted in here:

"Marcus, those bunds were built by the Portuguese. Jesuits were also farmers and engineers. The villagers are not maintaining them properly now. Anyway, they have planned a dozen canals for the southern region. The new governor has big plans. I have read a report in the Portuguese journal. The report spoke of many things that didn't exist in Europe in earlier days but are there now."

"And then it will be a land of milk and honey umh? Perhaps Prof. Leitão told you that. You are an intelligent boy, but don't trust those Portuguese bulletins too much. It may be happening in Europe but not in Portugal, anyway, it's too late for them," Marcus snorted, "let's move now," he added

The foothill they walked on had sparse plantation; the trees were cashew, Sal, and some shrubs with black berries.

"Stalin? Are you taking us to a rendezvous or what?" asked Caitu

"I like it when you address me by name. As socialists, we treat young boys as our comrades. Well, don't you feel the breeze blowing down the hill refreshing? It has put a spring in our walk."

A gust of stink made them turn sideways where a couple of jackals stood guard near an earth dug out.

"Let's see what's in there; make sure it's not a human," said Caitu. Even as the boys made a dash, the jackals didn't flinch on the other side. Looking down they saw more jackals and vultures jostling to feast on what was left of a dark carcass. Caitu remarked:

"I think a wayward calf had fallen in the stone quarry." The boys walked back and joined the mentors.

As Stalin and Caitu walked ahead Marcus slowed down illustrating to Bruno about the landscape they passed by:

"Down here is the adjacent low-lying field beside Baga; so it becomes the Baga lake in the monsoons. Baga is a ward of Velem; behind Baga is Murida, a ward of Kunkali; next to it is your Bandar, a ward of Osnem. The low lying field at Bandar becomes the Bandar lake."

He walked quietly and stopped by a tree: "And this Sal tree marks the end Velem and the start of Kunkali," he added

"Why weren't the villages and wards divided in proper order? And how can a tree be a marker? It will die one day," Bruno countered

"Look, a wayside tree was an ideal marker for the simple village folks to guide a passer-by. Villages evolved with human settlements and were shaped and re-shaped through conquests, re-conquests, land grabs by tribes or bequests by conquerors. This current geographical division isn't much different from what the Portuguese took over except the Latin twist they gave to our place names: *Bhag to* Baga, *Ad nuim to* Adnem, *Bandar* to Banda, Osnem to … well, you know it." He rambled on and resumed after a short pause:

"Another change they did was to transfer temple properties to the Church. This act could be termed both legal and illegal depending on how you look at it. It is illegal because it was made by the conquerors; it could be termed legal because the inheritors were our own people who willy-nilly converted. But the Portuguese did a lot more that wasn't right. They are trying to make amends now when it is too late. Had you been to Pandava cave any time?" He ended with a poser.

"Yes, once as a kid with a group of adults, boys and girls, for a picnic. We ate and drank outside the cave. They had planned to have a dance in the cave and had carried a gramophone player. But there was a lot of animal excreta inside so they had to dance outside," said Bruno with a chuckle

"Oh, a ballroom dance by the Pandava cave! Further up there on the hill is the *Shantadurga* temple.

I know men from Bandar go there during the *jatra* festival and dance with the umbrella which belongs to their ancestral clan. Even I do, as my father came from that clan too. The temple hill is where the devotees had fled to with their deities faced with a ruthless persecution during the Inquisition? Did you know who the most loyal supporter of the Inquisition was? Some say he who is most worshipped here…… " Bruno cut in raising his hand:

"Marcus, let's not dig old graves; history is full of them. I could also ask you: will you or Stalin change your name and religion? I am sure both of you will not. So all is well that ends well. Hindus have come back with their deities; they worship in their temples and work with the government. My father and mother are both devout Catholics. But they have no objection to those who partake in their ancestral rituals; and me too."

"You are an intelligent and level-headed boy. I wish you well in these troubled times. Dr. Salazar is aware of the blood-stained past of his forefathers and wants to make amends. But he is on his last leg. The Portuguese must leave or they will be kicked out. Well boy, let's catch up with our comrades who have gone ahead," said Marcus and they hurried on

Nearing the cave Stalin and Marcus moved to the front; a man who had sat under a tree pointed them towards the cave. Sheaves of browned grass overhung its roof casting a shadow across its entrance.

Inside three men had sat cross-legged facing the gate; the man in the centre had his head half hidden under a cap. Two boys who had sat opposite sprung to their feet imploring Stalin and Marcus to squat and exited the cave.

"A good day, Stalin and Marcus; comrade Naique welcomes you; on his left is Kishu, our young firebrand," said the man on the right

"Good day to comrade Naique, to you Juju and Kishu," chanted Stalin as Marcus murmured nodding his head. Naique lifted the cap revealing his gray head as he exchanged a few words with Juju. Then Juju spoke:

"Our comrade, the GFP secretary has come a long way under great risk. He will speak to you shortly. Well, you surely heard of our co-villager, Kishu. Now, the Secretary has assignments for you. He feels not much is happening at your end." He paused to add:

"Before we proceed, tell me about the two boys you brought here. Are they going to work for us? One looks like a kid to me."

"They are young but helpful, Juju. The tall one is my nephew Caetano. He had been a great help to me, running little errands, handing out pamphlets or passing on messages. He is an ace cyclist which helps too. We need not push them as they're still in school. You know how their mothers whimper," griped Stalin

After Naique spoke to him again, Juju resumed:

"Great! No contribution is too little to our fight Stalin. Good to catch them young. There are some new leaflets especially printed in our language in Roman script by GFP. Our comrade will talk to you and Marcus. But for now, let the boys have a little outing. You and Marcus may squat."

Marcus ushered Caitu and Bruno out speaking politely: "Hang around for a while or go pick some *boras*, our Goan plums. Don't go down to the village or speak to anyone. The boys outside will tell you when to come."

Seeing the two off, Marcus went back into the cave.

The man they had met earlier had shifted his post. He was sitting on a rock smoking a cigarette while the two boys had taken his place. As Caitu passed by the rock the man spoke to him between his puffs:

"What happened?......and this bulky bag you're carrying what for?

"They asked us to leave. We brought something to eat and drink. Stalin had brought us here for a picnic," said Caitu

"A picnic? But you don't eat meat here, especially beef that you people are fond of," he said sternly

"We just have egg sandwiches and water. Tell me, are there any *bora* trees here?" asked Caitu

"Quite a few but further up. But don't go back to the cave until you're called," he snapped

"Why are you sitting here?" asked Caitu

Annoyed, the man dismissed him pointing vaguely to the direction they should go. They clambered up and down circling between jutting boulders, sandy mounds and cashew trees, at times stopping to pick the wild berries. There were beaten paths to walk between patches of tall dried grass. When they finally found the *bora* tree, they had lost sight of cave. Caitu's eyes lit up.

"Just look up at the bloom, a thousand ripened tangy gooey plums! What luck no loafers passed this way!" He put his bag down and pulled a little cloth bag from it:

"No loafers and what are we Caitu?" snapped Bruno

"Never mind; it includes us. Hold the bag Bruno and watch how I shake the branches and bring down a hailstorm of *boras*. Put them all in, ripened and un-ripened ones," he exulted as he climbed up the tall gangly shrub just like him. Then standing at the central node he let his long arms shake every available branch till the tree was shorn of all its ripened fruits.

When Caitu got down, Bruno was still picking the *boras*. When they had scooped all up, the bag was half-full. They sat down to chat chewing away the sweet sour plums spitting out the seeds. When Bruno checked his watch an hour and a half had gone by.

"They haven't called us yet. But we have come a long way from the cave. Caitu, your uncle tricked us. Was this a picnic? Why are you pulling me along into this?" Bruno was visibly irritated.

"Sorry Bruno; I really thought it was a picnic when he asked mama for extra sandwiches. I will be careful next time. I will shout at him. Let's go home now," said Caitu giving Bruno a pat on the back

When they retraced their way back they found the two boys and the man missing. At the rock where the man had sat Caitu broke in:

"I am thirsty and hungry too. Let's sit down and recharge ourselves. Don't know when they're going to finish." Caitu cut short alerted by a shout from inside the cave.

"Caitu, I heard someone shout *'burro tonto'*, a silly ass," Bruno exclaimed with alarm

"It is the police. Let's run across the roof of the cave," Caitu whispered pulling Bruno along

"Venha aqui, apresse" hollered a tall *mestiço* as he strode out of the cave even as two uniformed policemen surged forward. The younger one with a shotgun closed in on them. The *mestiço* who had pulled out his revolver stood back.

"Come here quick," said the policemen with a shotgun in the local tongue. The boys moved over and the senior police who wore a badge and a revolver took over:

"Put your bag down and open it and then tell me who you are and what you're doing here," he yelled

Caitu was distracted. The *mestiço* who stood behind was twirling his revolver round his forefinger and aiming it over their heads looking angry.

Having checked the bag the inspector asked for their personal details noting it in a diary. From the same diary, he pulled out a sheet, unfolded it and held it before Bruno:

"Boy, have a good look at these two rows of photos. Do you recognize or seen any of these men? Bruno glanced at the sheet closely:

"I haven't seen nor recognize anyone in the photos," he said calmly

He told him to stand aside and turned to Caitu:

"What is your name?"

"Caetano Silva," said Caitu a bit nervously

"Caetano Santolino Silva is your name. You must surely recognize someone here. If we find you're lying, we will take you away. Our jeep is parked down the road." His tone was stern.

Before looking into the sheet, Caitu stole a glance at *mestiço* who sneered, aiming his revolver toward him.

"Don't you recognize anyone from the photos? You must know someone if he is from your village," shouted the officer. Caitu was visibly shaken as Bruno watched him calmly.

"Speak the truth and we won't trouble you." The tone was polite this time.

"I recognize one in the bottom row," said Caitu

"Point him out and tell who he is to you," the inspector shot back

"This one; he is Santolino, my uncle and godfather," said Caitu

"And still you say you don't know the others in the photo; two are his colleagues. You were once caught with pamphlets. I had questioned you, do you remember?" asked the officer

The *mestiço* ended his gunplay and ambled towards the inspector: *"Levante-o! Vamos interrogar esse vagabundo,"* he barked out and walked away towards the mud road

"Nephew of Stalin, you have to come with us. Let the other boy go home," said the officer pulling Caitu by the hand

"Where are you taking him and what should I tell his mama? We were here on a picnic. You've checked the bag," Bruno pleaded tailing the inspector

"Tell his mama we've taken him for questioning about his uncle. When we're done, we will reach him home. Tell her not to worry. You take the bag and go," the officer retorted firmly

"But he is thirsty and hungry. Let him take this bag," mumbled Bruno

"Alright, give him his bag." Then he asked Caitu to move.

A despondent Bruno ran back the way they had come and found Caitu's mama sitting in the balcony.

"Where is Caetano?" she asked as he climbed up the steps

Bruno narrated the dramatic tale. As he concluded she began:

"I don't know what this man, Stalin is up to. I suspected something when he suddenly appeared and talked about a picnic. He is not a man who goes on picnics. But to involve you school boys in his activities is a crime. Neither my son nor I know about his activities or with whom he is involved. We hear from others that he is a freedom fighter. So what else can Caetano tell the police about him? I am afraid they might treat him badly and even torture him. He's already in a depression since his sister's death. His father will be outraged if he hears about this. I am sorry they pulled you into this mess. If they don't bring him by afternoon, I will go there myself. Oh my God," she whined

"Nothing will happen to Caetano, auntie. The two local police weren't so bad. Only the half Portuguese man appeared threatening. He was playing with his pistol and aiming it over our heads as we stood there. I think he was trying to scare us. If you happen to go just remember we told them we were there on a picnic, just Caetano and me. Don't you mention we went with Stalin? Well, I will go home now."

"I understand, but Bruno, you must have lunch before you go. You must be thirsty too. It was kind of you to speak to the policeman the way you did and leave the bag behind," she said

"I will have some water but I will go home for lunch. I have a bicycle. It will take 15 minutes if I take the interior route." As Bruno turned she caught him by the hand and gave him a tight hug and a peck "Thank you, my son, you are an angel," she moaned

The short interior route had its own pitfalls for a cyclist in a hurry; a sandy path or a couple of stone steps up and down the way. Bruno was more worried than hungry.

CHAPTER VII

Caetano visits Bruno's house

School was to resume in a few days. Bruno and mother were seated in their verandah when they saw a cyclist riding across the mid bund. Bruno recognized him as he climbed up the stone steps lifting his bicycle. He rode along the sand path and reached the house. Placing the bicycle by the balcony wall, he came up the steps.

"Caitu, you surely know there's a better access from the bund road. I had shown it to you last time," said Bruno

"I know, but at the chapel, a little boy pointed out to go this way," he said

"Aha! Little boy is a little boy," Bruno laughed and introduced him to his mother.

"Mãe, this is Caetano from Velem, my new classmate this year."

Greeting him Ana posed the mundane queries the women folk were prone to ask after meeting someone from the neighboring village; his father's name, surname and what he did and then probed further about the siblings and other relatives. Then she went in.

"What happened to you? You have bruises on your knees?" asked Caitu

"A muscle pull and a bruised knee; I fell off my bicycle, riding over a stony path. I couldn't walk for a week. But I was worried about you. What happened later?"

"Oh me? Down the road, they pushed me into a jeep. *Mestiço* himself was at the wheel. He drove fastand rough making the jeep grunt like a buffalo. He was also yelling at the inspector: *'é merda, é merda, Cipriano.'* At the Kunkali outpost, the inspector questioned me again while the *mestiço* sat facing me. His right hand was resting on his thigh; it held a revolver.

At first, the questions were about Stalin; when he arrived and where and with whom he goes? They showed me the same photos, of Marcus, Juju and Kishu, and three more, one of whom was the gray head we saw at the cave.....well you saw them too, Bruno ..." Caitu stopped short as Bruno's mother came out with drinks.

"Have it, Caetano. It's refreshing. It's Vimto, Bruno's favorite." She smiled and went in as Caitu resumed.

"My answers were frank and swift: *Stalin rarely comes to our house and I don't know where or with whom he goes or what he does; Marcus, I see him sometimes in the bazaar; I have heard of Kishu and Juju but don't know them; the three GFP men in the photo, I don't know them from Adam."* Bruno jumped in grinning:

"You did well! And then they let you off."

"Let me off? The son of a devil, *mestiço* put his revolver to my head saying I am born liar. That son of a b..... kept yelling *'Ah merda....este bastardo é um mentiroso.'*

He also gave bad words in our tongue. I thought he would blow me off. But to my luck, someone walked in with a message and he rushed off barking abuses on his way out. He also took away our bag of *boras*. I could hear the jeep as it roared off. He didn't come back. That bloody son of a b..." Caitu's temper and voice were rising.

"Keep your voice down Caitu. My mother can hear you. She doesn't like bad words. I haven't even spoken to her about the incident. So how and when did they let you off?" asked Bruno keeping his voice low

"I was tense until mama turned up. I was asked to sit out during her questioning. I was called in again. As I entered the room, the inspector ranted on: *'Stalin must surrender immediately or he would be arrested and might even be shipped to Portugal. And you, this would be your last warning,'* he ended glaring at me. He cautioned mama to be extra vigilant about me. Then we were let off."

Later mama told me he asked her the same questions. Our answers couldn't be different; I used to often hear her speak to the police." Bruno signaled him to stop.

"You were smart there. Now have your drink. By the way, the police were casual with me when they showed me the photos."

"I know you're a clever boy. Stalin is my uncle and godfather too. I carry his name and surname. It is a huge burden on me. Though he tries to be honest about his cause he remains dishonest with his ways with us. I find him utterly foolish at times," Caitu snickered

"I think you should keep away from it all. Finish your school first. You've already lost two years. My father was about to send me to Belgaum. He thinks things are getting worse here. But my mother doesn't want me to leave her and go. As for me, I like the laidback life here. I enjoy the daily routine: get up early, go to the chapel, then to school; then play football in the evening. Study a bit under the oil lamp or tune in to Radio Ceylon, BBC, VOA and of course to our own *Emissora de Goa*. Once in away, more exciting things do happen, like the *teatro* in the bazaar square or a film show at the church. Then there are more exciting things like the last week's incident at the cave. Oh No! That's serious stuff and I don't want a repeat of it," he chuckled as his mother came to the door and said it was time for *canji*.

"No, I don't like that rice soup much. I will go home now. There's no news about Stalin. The police who used to visit us have stopped coming. May be they nabbed him. I will see you at school in a couple of weeks Bruno," he said and walked down to his bicycle

"Of course, you will," replied Bruno

After Caitu had left, Bruno went in and sat down at the table for a bowl of *canji*.

"What kind of a companion you have Bruno? I heard him using foul language every few seconds. And he was talking about police questioning him. What is going on Bruno?

You better keep away from this boy who seems much older to you. If your father hears of it, he might arrange to move you out of here," his mother cried out

"It's nothing mãe; he was talking about his uncle who is a freedom fighter."

"Freedom fighter? What's his name?" she snapped back

"Santolino alias Stalin."

"Well, I've heard that name Stalin. I will find out from Matilda," she grumbled

"Forget it, mãe. His uncle is only a supporter of freedom fighters. My father talks of Gandhi too. And Caetano has nothing to do with his uncle. He is from a different house. That boy is quite good at heart and helpful. I think he is affected by his sister's death. His mama looks sad. Ann Marie was her daughter too. I feel for his mama. Oh, I wish I had a sister."

"Oh really Bruno, you feel for his mama so much. So what about me? And you are now blaming me for not giving you a sister," she moaned in a mocking tone

"But I am warning you, Bruno. Your father has just left but he keeps in touch with affairs over here through his friends. He keeps many things to himself and acts suddenly. He has warned you already. You better keep away from this boy."

"I never blamed you mãe. Let's close the matter," Bruno reassured her with a peck on the cheek

His mother became quiet and thoughtful.

CHAPTER VIII

The School Resumes

By May end the rain clouds loomed over turning the air hot and humid. The maiden shower was abrupt but gentle, giving off a fragrance of its first kiss of the good earth. For days the rain fell in pauses until it announced its arrival with great thunder and lightning. Season in and season out, it never skipped its thunderous home coming and exit.

A week of incessant rains flooded the low lying wards and mud roads forcing the school to remain shut for three straight days as many students didn't turn up.

"Bruno, there had never been such a deluge in our lifetime. I think we might drown in the flood if it doesn't stop," moaned his mother

Then as the school resumed Caitu didn't turn up for a week. The day he turned up, Bruno fired a flurry of queries as they exited the classroom for the recess.

"What happened to you? Were you in some trouble? Has your uncle come back?"

"I will tell you; let's walk up to the monument under my umbrella; it's only a drizzle," he said.

With a drizzle outside, most girls stayed indoors. Boys with rainwear ventured as far as the river bank to pee. The gated monument a stone-throwaway offered the closest sit-out if the rains weren't heavy. Bathed by a drizzle it looked magnificent. From its centre rose a towering statue of Christ the King. A wide circular podium surrounded the plinth of the monument; around the podium stood the four apostles on stone pillars. A wall of stone and iron railings with four gates encircled the monument.

The boys got in unlatching the gate facing the school and climbed up the steps on to the podium.

"Let's sit on this step between Mathew and John," said Bruno

"Let's go sit at the back between the other two," Caitu countered. Going round at the back he pulled Bruno to sit below the plinth of the statue instead, and began:

"Stalin came home in the evening the day I came to your house, all bruised. He told us he was nabbed a week earlier in the bazaar and taken to the military camp. *Agente Menezes* grilled him for two days accusing him of helping GFP to plot against the state; he could be the same one we had met. He brandished a lit cigarette to Stalin's face, a few times before brushing it out on his thigh. Stalin denied having met or seen GFP men even as a soldier whipped him.

Menezes then dangled a gold bar before him, saying it will be his if he led him to a GFP senior. Stalin knew it was a trap. He didn't budge even as they lashed him for another day.

Finally they asked him if he was a freedom fighter. He told them he merely sympathized with his people seeking better education and jobs for their children and a reasonable free speech. They let him off with a warning; that he will be closely watched and will be shipped to Portugal next."

As Caitu concluded Bruno shook his head in disbelief:

"He told you all this and you felt sorry for him? Didn't he apologize for what he put you through?"

"And for what he put you through Bruno; mama confronted him about it. He said sorry with folded hands and swore such a thing won't happen again. He told me to say sorry to you."

Caitu stopped short as the gate screeched behind amid giggles. It had also stopped drizzling. Bruno got up.

"Let's go Caitu; the girls have sneaked in." Coming round they found the girls sitting on the steps talking in hushed tones.

"Where you two are running off, to the river to pee? Go run before you wet the pants; the bell is about to ring," quipped one as others cackled

"Careful Cecilia, don't tell bad jokes or love stories. Christ the King is above and down below are the four evangelists; you are under watch," snapped Caitu. The giggling petered out as the boys walked away.

"Stalin tells me the evangelists might not be the writers of the gospels because they didn't sign the gospels,"

Caitu remarked

"Don't fall for Stalin's remarks about gospels. Those works have been researched by scholars."

"And do you know those scholars Bruno? You must question when you are in doubt."

"What does it matter? What is written there is the very essence of Christianity. Let's not discuss it further," Bruno snapped back

"Good boy. I will try and stick to your advice."

As they neared the school the bell rang signaling the end of recess.

By June end the low lying fields had turned into ponds and seasonal lakes. Two weeks on, Caitu again did not report to school for three straight days. The school received a note that he had a knee injury. Bruno told his mother about it and by the weekend he decided to go and see him.

"I might stay over for the night if need be," he said

"If need be? Are you a doctor or a nurse Bruno? His mother is there. And tomorrow is a Sunday. You have to attend the service at the chapel," she protested

"Mãe, I'm not the only boy in the village; there is sacristan and few other boys. I already spoke to the chaplain. I will hear mass at the Velem church. It isn't far from his house."

"Oh! So you planned it all. I don't know what to say," she protested

That evening Bruno set out with an umbrella, cutting through adjoining wards. Unable to cut through a water-logged field he detoured and got on the high bund road. He could see Xapo on one side. It was truly a lake now. Reaching the church Bruno was shocked to see Caitu playing football in the open space by the cemetery. Through a gentle sun shower the boys continued playing as Bruno watched from the sideline. When the match ended, Caitu greeted him:

"Glad to see you Bruno."

"While the class prayed for you to get well soon, I see you playing football," quipped Bruno

Caitu sniggered: "Oh! Is it? Even when I'm so notorious? Let us go home now."

As they walked Caitu rambled: "With the rains our ponds and rivers have bred lots of fish. I have been fishing with guys for three straight days and coming home late in the evening with loads of fish. After supper, I would retire into our sitting room, play a few records and then pick up my banjo that I had dumped. I would play and sing past midnight even as mama kept yelling from her room reminding me of the school next day. Come morning, I just couldn't get up. I had a headache too." Bruno broke in:

"So you sent a sick note to school faking a knee injury. And your mama kept quiet?"

"Mama had objected to it from day one. Last evening when I came home she flung out my catch and then she cried. I promised her I will not go again."

"Hope you will keep up your promise."

"I will Bruno. Now, you came at the right time. Just this morning a boat owner, my papa's friend, came with a bagful of shrimps. He brings it to us every monsoon."

"Must be solar shrimps, a delicacy; you get them plenty with the onset of monsoon," said Bruno

"Good, mama has marinated and kept aside for you. I had told her you would come. Make sure you stay over till tomorrow lunch time. Another thing, this evening we are meeting a famous doctor at Urbano's house; the doctor who lit the first spark of freedom movement in the village. Urbano supports the freedom fighters on the quiet. He says the doctor is a peaceful man and likes to motivate the youth. I heard he is very humorous too."

"I thought the doctor is barred from entering the territory. And how you know this Urbano?" asked Bruno

"My papa knows Urbano as he works in a shipping company. But papa doesn't support their movement."

"Caitu, I remember Leitão spoke of him as a communist like your uncle," said Bruno

"You need not worry about that. No Stalin or doctor can influence you. But this is a rare opportunity that has come our way. Let's go and meet the doctor," said Caitu

As they reached Caitu's house the drizzle petered off and the skies brightened. Filu and Marta were standing in the front yard. Filu seemed quite cheerful.

"Bruno, where have you been? I wish you were older, but I can still wait for you," she blurted

"Filu, don't you feel ashamed now that you're engaged," snapped Caitu

"I'm only joking Caitu. You know I get a thrill embarrassing shy boys." She walked away giggling

"Come Bruno, good to see you," said Marta smiling. As the three walked up the steps, Caitu turned round:

"Mama, Bruno is staying home for the night,"

"He is always welcome," she said and gave him a hug and went in. Caitu told Bruno to sit saying he would be back after a wash. Marta came back with tea and biscuits. She spoke in haste:

"Good that you've come. The whole of last week Caetano hasn't gone to school. He has been going fishing with big guys and coming home late. After a hurried meal he would lock himself up in the sitting room, play the gramophone and then play the banjo and sing well past midnight. I would shout reminding him of the school. Come morning, I would find him lying on a mat in deep sleep. When I talked of school, he would tell me he isn't feeling well. By noon he seemed to be fine. Did he send a sick note to school Bruno?" Before Bruno could answer Caitu walked out:

"Shall we go Bruno?"

"Where are you taking him Caetano? No fishing, I told you," Marta shouted

"Mama, we're not going fishing. We're going to see a doctor at Urbano's house."

"Good, for once you're doing what is beneficial. See that he checks you properly. Tell him everything, your headaches, tiredness and what not." She tried to walk in but stopped at the doorway looking at her son:

"Yes mama, I shall tell him everything," said Caitu

Relieved, she turned and walked inside.

"Let's move Bruno. It has stopped drizzling. It is only about two kilometers from here. It is the one of the three farthest wards of our village and has its own church."

CHAPTER IX

A rendezvous with the doctor

Asking Bruno to hop on the back seat Caitu pedaled along the sandy road. Cutting behind the church he passed through a narrow bazaar lane, where he responded to a couple of greets from his pals. He turned on to a wider bund-road lined by palms and squares of paddy fields. The road bifurcated across a cemetery in a field. Caitu gave a rundown:

"For lack of space they built this cemetery in the field; it serves the three farthest wards of Velem. The road to the right will take you down to the farthest ward where Sal flows by. As the river reaches the mouth it turns languid because the sea only swallows it in little gulps."

"Oh, you are a good story teller too; many talents you have Caitu," quipped Bruno

Caitu turned left onto a bund path that led to a patch of garden land of fruit trees and palms sheltering houses at random. Their trail ended when Caitu halted by a modest house with a small verandah covered with coco mats on either side. As Caitu put his bicycle on the stand, Bruno noticed two bicycles by a mango tree:

"One bicycle looks like Stalin's, and I can see a road ahead by the foothill. Caitu, I hope you haven't brought me to a rendezvous with Stalin's gang," Bruno grumbled
"Stalin knows Urbano but we haven't come here to see him" said Caitu pushing in through the front door.

They heard voices behind a door to the left. Caitu knocked and pushed in pulling Bruno along. The voices fell silent resonating the tick-tock of the clock on the rear wall that had a door. The windows of the room were shut.

A graying middle-aged man was seated between Marcus and Stalin on a sofa. With a wide grin on his scratched face, Stalin strode across and put a hand on Bruno's shoulder:

"I am sorry for what happened last time. Someone snitched on us. Good you came; this is a lifetime opportunity to meet our mentor, who kindled the first spark of freedom in this village. I was as young as you then." He leaned towards the rotund graying man.

"Doctor, these boys have shifted from Portuguese to English school. The Portuguese promoted their own language suppressing our native tongue. They made Christians study in Portuguese and pray in Latin while Hindus could pray and study in their tongue. Now, the Portuguese schools are being displaced by English schools."

"Well, leave aside the language; it's only a tool of communication. Let's talk of freedom that is dear to us. I hear folks here have sunk into a state of submission and lethargy. Parents tell their children to devote to church and school saying fight for freedom is dangerous business as one can get jailed or shot. Now what can I do for these boys?" asked the doctor smiling

"The two are intelligent boys. Caetano is my nephew; he has done a few errands for me. Bruno the younger one has an open mind. Now that they're here I want you to enlighten them about what freedom really means. I mean your socialist ideals."

Stalin asked boys to pull up the chairs and sit as a man walked in through the rear door.

"Caetano, good you came. Your papa is my good friend though he doesn't support our movement. And who is this boy?"

"He is the son of Roque from Bandar, a Gandhi follower," Marcus cut in. Urbano shook hands with Bruno and turned round:

"Doctor, I need to see a lawyer regarding an affidavit. His house is across the river. As Marcus and Stalin know their way around I am taking them with me. We will be back soon. If you need anything, just call out to Remetina. I told her to stay alert."

"Well, I will wait as we have issues to sort out. And Stalin, please keep an eye and your ears pricked up to anything unusual you see or hear around our place. You know I cannot move about freely, though I am not active. Now that India is done with the constitution and has become a republic, some hardliners are pressing Nehru and he's turning the screw on Salazar. Salazar's secret police is turning the screw on us," the doctor ended with a mock chuckle

As the three walked away, Stalin gave a parting shot:

"Caetano, the boat ride is confirmed for tomorrow. There will be a group of boys. It's going to be a fine sunny day. Get Bruno if he's around. Be at the fisherman's wharf by 8 O'clock. Boatman Amrut will be there. Only bring water to drink. You will be treated to a lavish lunch. Treat Bruno well."

"You should have told me earlier. How did you know we are coming here and that it will be a sunny day tomorrow?" Caitu shot back

"Urbano told me you're coming; the weatherman on the radio said it will be a sunny day. See you boys!" He replied as he waved out and walked off.

As they departed the doctor got to talking. He asked the boys where their fathers worked and then about their school and their future plans. Caitu said he would join a ship and Bruno spoke of his plan to go to Africa. The wide grin turned wider:

"So, you both wish to go away leaving your home and family. You also left the Portuguese school and joined an English School."

"We would love to live with our family in our own land. But there are no jobs nor good training institutes or colleges here. Men from our villages have been leaving since my grandpa's time to work or study in Indian cities. There are opportunities in Africa too. We are lucky to have an English school that will prepare us to take up jobs in India or Africa," enthused Bruno.

"So young men, what then is the purpose of the Portuguese ruling over us? They can neither give you jobs nor good education nor your freedom. And why should you go and work in Africa and deprive the poor natives of an opportunity." As the boys didn't answer he fired a query.

"Are you good Christians?"

"We do our religious duties regularly. We are altar boys. I serve at the chapel while he serves at the church," said Bruno enthusiastically, anticipating doctor's approval, if not an applause

"Did I ask you about going to church? Do you think going to church or being an altar boy makes you a good Christian? Or does going to the temple or mosque make one a good Hindu or Moslem? Or, does meditating in a Buddha pose make one a Buddhist?"

"Doctor, it is not for us to judge others; they will be judged by God as our religion has taught us," uttered Bruno

"Sensible answer, you have been well trained by the priests," quipped the doctor as Caitu jumped in:

"Doctor, are you a communist or socialist? People say you are a communist. They say the same of my uncle Stalin who claims you were his mentor. He says things like *religion is the opium of the people*' and *'workers of the world unite'. "* Flashing an inscrutable stare, the doctor responded:

"Caetano, you seem like a busy body in the village. But it's good that I've met you because at least I know people talk about me. Listen, Christ message says '*love others as much as you love yourself and feed the poor and the needy.*' Was he a socialist or a communist? Moreover if the priest says I am a communist then I am anti-church and if Prof. Leitão says it then I am both anti-church and anti-Portuguese. I am neither answerable to them nor affected by what they say. But I am critical of priests for their own sins and their silence over the rulers' wrongdoings. I am also not answerable for Stalin's views and actions even if he claims that I was his mentor. The terms, like '*religion is the opium of the masses*' or '*workers of the world unite*' are clichés of communism; merely reciting these slogans and not going to church doesn't make one a communist or a socialist. But to '*workers of the world unite*' I would add '*faiths and nations of the world unite*'." Bruno made an interjection:

"Doctor, I can relate to you many instances of unity of faiths. In my village, Hindu women wait by the wayside to kiss the image of St. Sebastian. They believe Sebastian was a Hindu before he became Christian. Likewise, on Good Friday the Hindu men in our bazaar close their shops and stand in silence as the procession carrying the crucified Jesus and the grieving Mother Mary pass by. We Christians sit on the Hindu *pedd* around the banyan tree and their boys sit at our monument. Also, Bandar villagers donate towards the temple and a few of our men attend the Hindu *jatra* festival and do their Umbrella Dance at the hill temple." Before he could finish Caitu cut in:

"In my village Hindu women light candles at the cross and kiss the glass case of Mother Mary's image believing she is one of their Devis. They have many Devis. We have one Mother Mary and yet the Protestants and some other Christians don't venerate Mary but only Jesus. I don't know who is holier." Bruno shushed him:

"Caitu, forget about them. Mother Mary is the one and only, the kind and forgiving mother who intercedes on our behalf. The Hindu Devi comes in various forms of womanhood." The doctor raised a finger to intercede:

"Bruno, you mean in different avatars of a deity: the powerful, the angry and vengeful, the wise, the bountiful, the artist, the musician; or the mother, wife, sister, daughter and so on. That seems realistic to me too reflecting the organic world. You two seem like the ego and alter ego of each other. I too went through such battles in my growing years. And Bruno, the instances you cited is not the sort of unity of faiths I had meant. All faiths have faults because they were made by man and it is human to err. What I meant was the steps or principles born out of an enlightened mind. That is doubtful as man is also part of the beast. He has a warring and tribal instinct. Now, let's keep aside matters of faith lest I be accused of corrupting the young minds. Tell me about the present situation here. Freedom fighters are complaining that people here are not coming out in support of their cause." Bruno was quick to respond:

"Doctor, at the moment we in the territory are better off as far as social justice. Our women have more freedom and also property rights. There has never been a dispute between the two religious communities. We rarely hear of robberies or murders and people are not dying of sickness or hunger as in other parts of India. Even the prisoners are fed well by the Portuguese. No wonder then freedom fighters do not get mass support. People don't want to go to jail. How then will you motivate a young man to be a freedom fighter? Also, at the border the Indian guards hassle us a lot more than the Portuguese." Bruno cut short as doctor raised a finger.

"Young man, you sound like the spokesman of Prof. Leitão. I might be out of touch with the present situation here and I am also not representing the Indian government. I know its task is huge considering the large population with ethnic, caste and religious divisions." He cleared his throat and resumed:

"Now you say people are not hungry and yet you complain of a few hardships imposed by the Indian government. Your fathers work for Indian shipping companies and many others work or study in Indian cities. So you cannot say the Portuguese are feeding you. The rest of India accepts you because you are geographically and culturally linked with them. So let us reunite and be a part of the new secular nation. It's a small sacrifice. You may have food in the belly but must have fire in the belly to fight for freedom. I don't expect you to be freedom fighters but at least do your bit by enlightening the folks around you." Bruno put up his hand:

"Well you also said *let the nations unite;* we have the United Nations, isn't it doctor?"

"It is a band of the victors who are playing two opposing political concertos and other tunes of conflict; as new nations emerge they will add their harmonic and disharmonic overtones and undertones. We will wait and see if they harmonize well," he chuckled

"I don't know what you mean by that, doctor," said Bruno

They were distracted as a woman showed up from the back door:

"Doctor, I've served tea and crackers with cheese for you and the boys. Please come in," she said

"Thank you Remetina, we're on our way." He got up: "let's go sit at the table boys. You can ask me questions but not while you're munching." He guffawed and shuffled across.

The woman directed the boys to the two side chairs and offered the doctor a high-backed chair with a cushion to sit on. He asked her to remove it.

Between sips of tea, Caitu fired a salvo:

"Doctor, I heard many years ago you and a few colleagues met an Indian leader in hiding followed by public meetings in town. The Portuguese beat up the locals one of whom was summarily tried and sent to Portuguese jail. The Indian leader was kicked out and you fled to an Indian city. I heard you are doing your bit there like issuing pamphlets. But couldn't you do more by being here?"

The doctor crunched harder at his cheese-cracker and took a deep gulp of his cup to swallow it. He smirked:

"Nephew of Stalin, your uncle tells me you were a great help to him. But now you are also mocking us. I cannot be critical of the regime here and earn my living. Though I am not actively involved now I am still considered as the enemy of the state. If they arrest me they might also ship me to Portugal. Our colleague that you spoke of has just been shipped back after languishing for eight years at the Peniche Fortress. He did not go there to be fed well as your friend spoke." Caitu spoke again in haste:

"Doctor, I want your say on a couple of issues that have been bothering me. Is it necessary to go to church or temple to pray? And can I convert to another religion if I am not happy with the religion I was born in?"

"Well that tells me something, a bit more than what I thought about you two. While Bruno has embraced the faith he was born into, you are searching answers after studying in a seminary school for three years. You are a complex individual. But I can tell you about me. I don't need to go to church or temple to pray. I don't pray your prayer.

And now to your next question; if you're not happy with the faith you were born in, you don't have to convert to another faith. You will jump into another soup. Just keep your belief to yourself and follow it quietly without coming into conflict with others."

Doctor cut short as the window beside him vibrated. Caitu put up his hand:

"Now doctor, a final query about the activists we have around here. Who amongst them is a real freedom fighter with fire in the belly? Stalin, Marcus, Juju or a GFP member or anyone that you know of?" he asked

There was a roar of a vehicle that instantly died off. A nervous Remetina quietly opened the back door to let a man in. He hurried towards the doctor:

"Doctor, Urbano has told me to shift you to his cousin's house. He said it is only a precaution as there was a police raid at your place. He doesn't know what they were looking for. He also told the two boys here to go home. Now, do you have any luggage to put in the car?"

The doctor pointed to a bundle and a bag; picking it up the man rushed out. The doctor picked up a rolled mat and started to leave; at the door, he turned round:

"Thank you Remetina! And boys, I've heard of one Kishu who could be the one with fire in the belly. But I don't know if he is the real one. Study more and read widely and enlighten yourself. Adeus!" he exclaimed and shuffled out from the back door

CHAPTER X

A night at Caetano's home

On their way home Caitu and Bruno were caught under a drizzle. As he cycled back home, Caitu reminded Bruno of the boat ride that Stalin talked about.

"I am wary of your uncle. You know what happened to us once. Do you still believe him?"

Bruno, Stalin has learnt his lesson; he knows they will pack him off to Portugal next. Also, Amrut doesn't get involved in freedom activities, and there will be other school boys."

"That's what he said. Why are you speaking for him? I don't trust Stalin, though I would love to go on a boat ride, " Bruno grumbled

They were quite wet when they reached home. Marta had heated a large pot of water.

The boys had their bath and Caitu gave Bruno shorts and a shirt. Marta then asked her son if the doctor had checked him.

"He did mama. He said there's nothing wrong with me." Bruno felt a pang of sadness watching mama's face. Then Marta served the dinner; chicken soup two side dishes of solar shrimps and roast chicken. Bruno waited to chat with her till she finished her meal.

Caitu then ushered Bruno into the sitting room. Marta came in and suggested they make their bedding.

"Shall I put a quilt over the mat for you Bruno? Caetano sleeps on a reed mat with two linen sheets and two pillows," she said

"Auntie, the same for me but only one pillow."

After making their bedding away from the centre table, she left the room. Then Caitu came with two mugs and a jug of water.

"Let me make for us a cool drink. It's right there in the cupboard, your Vimto. Mama bought a bottle as soon as I told her it's your favorite. I will have raspberry," he said opening a side door, displaying bottles of colorful concentrates.

"Really, so nice of your mama!" said Bruno

"She loves you more than me Bruno, mama's boy!" Caitu giggled

After pouring the drinks Caitu moved at the centre table. They sat there sipping their drinks. The bulbous chimney of the wick lamp dispersed the white orange flame all around.

"Tell me what do you think of the doctor? He was going back and forth. He thinks you need not be a churchgoer or altar boy to be a good Christian. That is for you Bruno. I like his slogans: *'faiths and nations of the world unite', 'the band of the victors'*, and *'political concertos'*. Do you agree with his ideas?"

"Before we talk about the doctor I am begging you to please stop troubling your mama. Don't you feel her pain Caitu? I swear I won't have anything to do with you if you don't change," snapped Bruno

"Do you think I don't feel her pain? Bruno, I am trying my best to remain sane for her."

"Then please stop lying to her all the time and change your ways. She is quite naïve Caitu and believes your bluffs. Now, the doctor might be a socialist or acommunist but also a simple man. Didn't you see he only carried a mat? I don't know what your uncle is? But I will not be influenced by them. Now play a record at low volume. Mama might have gone to sleep."

"Not yet; it's only about nine now. I know you like Ramona. I love it too." Caitu ambled to the gramophone with his glass in hand and played the record.

Coming back he peeped into Bruno's mug.

"Your mug is almost empty; let me make you another." After refilling Bruno's mug he took a swig of his own and rambled on.

"During the last few trips papa added to his collection, mostly American and Brazilian records. So we added bolero and samba to our dance collection, of foxtrot, waltz and swing. Sometimes, Filu and the neighbors would join us in the evenings. A single that Ann loved to dance and listen in her last days was *Rum and Coca Cola* by Andrew Sisters. After we were done with dancing I would strum my banjo and we would all sing our traditional folk songs. Finally, I would play and sing Ramona, with papa ending the refrain on a high note."

"Oh, a real family concert Caitu," said Bruno smiling

"There won't be a repeat," said Caitu taking more swigs of his drink as the disk played out

"Could you play Rum and Coca Cola by Andrew Sisters? I hear it on Radio Ceylon. Nice harmony," said Bruno

As Caitu strode towards the gramophone Bruno had a sip from his mug.

"Caitu, your drink has alcohol in it. Are you filching off your papa's bar?"

"You sniffing hound." Caitu frowned back at Bruno and then sniggered.

"I added a bit of what was left of the pint I had bought a week ago. It served me as a pick-me-up to get back to the banjo. I don't have the key to papa's bar. It remains locked when he is away," he ended with a girlish giggle

Bruno gave him a searching look as he sat down: "I got it; that's how you kept awake late and couldn't wake up in time."

After Rum and Coca Cola played out, Caitu closed the gramophone and brought out his banjo. He strummed a rhythm and hummed a tune. As Bruno leaned to watch his two hands move in different ways, Caitu paused in between to explain:

"To make simple chords like C, F, G, I only need two left hand fingers to press against the fret, say index and middle finger for C & F chords and index and ring finger for G chord. My right hand holds the plectrum to strum a rhythm or play a solo. But timing of music is like math too. With practice it becomes your pulse. At first I was awful. If you're interested, I will teach you while you teach me math."

"Indeed, I would love to. Talking of math, our math teacher is leaving the school; they are starting a new English school in my neighboring village next year."

"So you would surely shift to that school. I shall follow you there if you do," Caitu retorted

"I cannot say about next year. My father is bent on sending me to Belgaum though my mother is against it." Bruno turned thoughtful.

Caitu strummed and sang making Bruno to sing along, at times pausing to chat to keep him from nodding off. But Bruno was a day bird, early to sleep and early to rise. As the night wore on, he started to yawn.

"You may sleep Bruno. I would play for a while low and slow, and then come to sleep."

Bruno hit the mat and in minutes began to snore oblivious to the hum and strum. Caitu stopped humming and fiddled tremolo style. At one time, Bruno turned in his sleep as though distracted by the sound and mumbled: *'Oh Ramona. Even the tremolo sounds romantic. Keep playing.'*

"I think Ann Marie got fonder of it because papa and mama often danced to it. They also danced with Ann in papa's lap."

"How lovely it must have been?" said Bruno and turned over

Through the night Bruno woke up a few times. The first time he saw Caitu sitting and humming to himself to a low lingering strum. The second time he was awakened by a knock and saw Caitu pour from the pint into his glass. The last time he woke up it was raining hard and Caitu was snoring beside him.

CHAPTER XI

The boat ride

Bruno was a habitual pre-dawn riser. He remembered it was a Sunday. Later Caitu's mama walked in and opened the inner doors of the two front windows letting the morning light in. The sun did turn up. Caitu, still in deep slumber, had his legs stretched out of the mat.

"Bruno, good you're awake. There's a service at 8 and at 9. I wonder if this boy would get up at all. He's been doing this for days now; playing gramophone, then the banjo well past midnight and come morning he wouldn't get up," she muttered and raised her pitch:

"Caetano! Wake up. It is Sunday. Bruno is up and is waiting for you."

Caetano looked at mama with his eyes half-closed. He turned over to avoid her glowering face.

"I am tired mama. You go and take Bruno along," he mumbled. Marta walked away with a sullen face.

"What about the boat ride Caitu, the one Stalin spoke about?" asked Bruno

"The boat ride? Oh, It's raining," he groaned pulling a sheet over his head

Later that morning between two heavy showers the sun showed up again. By nine Bruno came home and found Caitu still lying down but awake.

"I am sorry Bruno. I think I went to sleep quite late. But you're wet. You could have used my raincoat," he said sitting up

"I had my umbrella. Got a little wet. It was a sharp diagonal passing shower. But the sun is out now. Caitu, I saw you pour into your glass from a pint. You've been drinking regularly. Do you need alcohol to play the banjo? You've been cheating and lying all along," Bruno snapped irritably

"Oh! It's not just the banjo. It also makes me relive the times I spent with my sister. I feel her presence in the room," he whimpered

"That's a mere excuse Caitu. I got a stale whiff the first day I met you. I thought you had a drink the previous evening. Then you had a drink within minutes at the bazaar when I went to the shop. You're an addict, Caitu," Bruno protested

"It's all over, I mean the pint. Let's not talk about it. Mama will be here anytime.
Now, let's have some coffee and eat something. Mama bakes the best bread with grated coconut and when you eat with salted Australian butter or a slice of Kraft cheese, it's irresistible. The coffee will be with *Cruz Azul* condensed milk, if the milkman did not turn up. Now and then he does that saying the calf stole the milk," he chuckled

"Oh, the boat ride, Stalin would be upset Bruno. He had been planning it for a month," Caitu stifled a yawn

"Is the boat waiting for you? He had told you to be there at eight."

"Don't worry! Amrut has many boats. He or his men would be around to take us where Stalin is. Let's be quick now. I will give you a swift ride," said Caitu jumping off the mat

As they sat for the breakfast, Marta returned and gave her son an earful:

"Caetano, the Vicar complained about you saying you didn't turn up for the children's catechism class, and also for the morning service for three days."

"But you did tell him mama that I wasn't well," he mumbled

"I did. But he said he saw you playing football in the afternoons," she shot back and added:

"And did you meet Stalin by any chance? He was planning to leave for Bombay with a passport but now he is stuck; I don't know for how long?"

"He can go whenever he wants to with or without passport. He is at Urbano's house."

"So you met him or you've been there. I know he keeps you informed of where he goes. Urbano is one of the few who hasn't kept away from him. Villagers don't want trouble. But they are a wonderful couple with kind hearts, he and sister Remetina," said Marta and walked away

After breakfast Caitu told Bruno to be in the same shorts he had worn overnight and gave him a pair of his papa's rubber shoes.

Then Caitu told his mama that they are going on a long bicycle ride to a friend's place.

"We will be eating lunch where we are going. You deserve some rest mama," he said

"Be careful Caetano; I hope you're not going to attend any of Stalin's secret meetings again. You can't rely on his promises. And mind you, don't take Bruno to the lake or river; they are swollen right now," she said sternly

"Mama, the house you grew up in, was just across the river bank. Certainly, you shouldn't be troubled by a swollen river so far away. He is safe with me. I can carry him on my back across the river or lake," he giggled

Minutes later Caitu set off on his bicycle with Bruno at the back. On his way seeing the Vicar in the front yard he cut from behind the cemetery and zoomed past from behind the church. After a few minutes Bruno said to him:

"We're going the same way we went yesterday. I hope you're not taking me to the doctor's safe house."

"Our route shall divert by the cemetery. I don't know where the doctor has gone."

At the cemetery Caitu took a right turn. "Last time I turned left. Now, we are passing through the hamlet of Kharxet, the field of salt. You can see fish or salt ponds around. All the late comers to Velem were pushed in here."

"Are you giving your own twist? My father's cousin is married in this village but they live in Belgaum. Our elders told me your villagers came from Carambolim after an epidemic. An elephant had fallen in the lake, and you guys never knew what made you sick," retorted Bruno with a chuckle

"Oh, that's a tribal twist given by your villagers. Though we live in peace, we do mock each other." Caitu snickered

After about a kilometer Caitu pedaled hard across a marshy stretch and got stuck in the mud. He got off the bike: "I shouldn't have braked; the ground is too muddy," he grumbled

They trudged the path reaching the river bank. Caitu kept peeping in passing by a row of huts where men were mending the nets. He stopped by a large hut. A man there acknowledged him.

"Are you Caetano, nephew of Stalin? Amrut left at eight with Stalin and other boys? If you are Caetano, go down and meet Sheikh Bullah, a bearded man waiting by his boat."

"Yes, I am Caetano; can I leave my bicycle here?"

"Just park it by that pole. Lock if you have to. Don't worry about it?" said the man

Walking along the bank Caitu spotted the boat with two men.

"I am Caetano," he said aloud

"Get in the boat and I will take you to your uncle," blurted the bearded man sizing up the boys

The boys hopped into the boat that swayed a little. It had one large triangular sail. Inside the boat there was a clutter of nets, cane baskets, peeled coconuts, rubber tubes and stems of banana plant.

"There's a gentle surface wind. Last two days the weather has been good. You two sit on the edge in the center facing each other. If you feel shaky you may squat down," said the man

"What's your name?" asked Caitu

"I am Sheikh Bullah and that is Pandu," he said pointing to his assistant who pushed the boat aside with a pole

They rowed the boat smoothly down the river until it met with a large sandbar near its mouth. From the east another stream flowed down to meet the sluggish Sal and the two flowed out as one between a narrow sandy peninsula and a hillock that shot into the sea gradually arching south. Sheikh and Pandu had taken to the oars to guide the boat through the channel. It picked up speed coming into the open sea under a drizzly wind.

Caitu looked sad of a sudden. "What is it Caitu?" asked Bruno

"I remembered Ann Marie. Can you see that thin conical strip of white sand? Stalin had brought me and Ann there; Ann called it the Little Finger Beach. She died a month later." Caitu whimpered. He turned to the boatman:

"Sheikh, where are you taking us? I thought Stalin would be at the beach."

"We are going much further, ahead of that Light House. You will find your uncle up there," he said curtly turning to his assistant; then the two chatted on.

Bruno nudged Caitu: "Look at the mast. He has put up two flags on his boat. I wonder what for?" he murmured. Sheikh turned round:

"Boy, I heard you; the wind picks up your whispers," said Sheikh raising his tone:

"The green is the fisherman's flag and the other one is a Portuguese flag. We are under their rule right now. Look up the hill. The naval comandante is watching us from the fort. He has binoculars. There's a huge cannon opposite the beach strip. Of course, it is not in use. But there are soldiers with guns.

And further down below you can spot a boat which can run faster than the wind. We have to identify ourselves for our safety. These waters have been trouble free but the naval police are alert these days. However, the *comandante* knows me too. I offer him king fish, the best of my catch with no blemish or scratch." Sheikh guffawed turning to his assistant.

An ideal wind direction made the two men's work easier. They only had to keep the boat away from low rocks. After a half hour journey they let the boat move towards a narrow sandbank between two little rocks. There was a country boat half resting on the land.

"You can see a little temple up there. There's a path that will take you there in ten minutes. Pick up a stick and beat around the bush as you go. It is helpful as there is fresh undergrowth along the path. There will be someone at the temple to tell you where Stalin is. You may leap off the boat now. I am sure you're both football players," said Sheikh grinning

Caitu took the water flask from Bruno and leaped well clear of the boggy patch. Bruno leaped short and his outsized shoes got stuck in the muck. He cleaned them at the water's edge.

His grin turning into a smirk, Sheikh turned the boat nudging the rock with the pole as he hollered over the whirring wind:

"Amrut will bring you home. They're all up there."

There were a few sticks lying around. The boys picked one each.

"As I beat left you try to sync with me beating on the right like you beat a crash cymbal," Caitu chuckled

They did it for a while. Further on, they found the path had been cleared off the outgrowth.

"Many boatmen and their families come this way to visit the temple. Up on the left there are a few mud houses and huts; one is Amrut's house. Stalin had taken me there once; I must have been about ten and Stalin about eighteen. Amrut doesn't live there now but goes there during the day," said Caitu

He stopped dead in his tracks alerting Bruno. A large reptile with dark brown patches with irregular golden rings on its skin crossed their path.

"It's a python Bruno and not a poisonous cobra," said Caitu aloud

"Be careful. Grandma told me you shouldn't take Cobra's or *Nag's* name," Bruno mumbled nervously

"Oh cobra, Nag, get out of our way," Caitu sniggered as the snake slithered into a bush.

"Don't believe in those tales? I heard stories from my granny too. She told me the *nagin* is a vengeful female cobra. Once a seaman on holiday tried to kill one but missed her. That night she slipped into his house and bit him while he was asleep," said Caitu

"The story I heard from my granny was even worse Caitu. The *nagin* followed her attacker to his ship by hiding in his steamer trunk and bit him when he opened it. They killed her but he too died. But do you think these stories are true?" asked Bruno

"I don't think so? The more faithful you are the more you believe in those stories, Stalin tells me."

They trudged on landing on an undulating plateau that met a patchy sky of grey, blue and milky white.

Bruno scanned the landscape heaving a sigh:

"There aren't any houses here. But there seems to be a road up ahead. And where is the temple Caitu?" he yelled

"I am also wondering where they all are? I hope it's not a hoax." He beamed as he turned round:

"Bruno, look to your left at the banana bunch; it's ripe for plucking. Let's cut if off. At least we will go home with bananas," he exclaimed

"And how do you plan to go home from here with the bunch?" asked Bruno

"I am here. I will take you home, but you can't pluck the bunch. There's someone in the hut down there," said the familiar voice. He was standing above a walled square yard a little away from a rectangular structure with a bonnet roof, the *ghumti*; the forlorn little shrine stood there overlooking the Arabian Sea.

"I was watching your boat from up here. But Caitu, I had told you to be at the wharf by eight. Your junior team boys suspect you are drinking on the quiet. Concentrate on your school and football. The seniors expect you to don the club jersey soon. Don't spoil your chances Caitu. Now, come up here and have a look," said Stalin

The boys had to enter the yard through the only opening and then leap over the low wall at the other end. As they came up Stalin pointed a finger to the scene beneath:

"Isn't it a beautiful sight? They say our territory is the most picturesque coastal strip on the west of the Ghats?"

Down below, the waves lashed the dark weathered rocks and further to the right lay the narrow strait. To the left the Little Finger beach merged with the main shore line of silver sands that extended over a dozen kilometers. Inland to the east were the slopes of Western Ghats.

"No wonder the Portuguese found it irresistible," quipped Caitu as Bruno responded

"Hindus believe our land was created by their god after shooting an arrow in the sea. But our priests say it is creation of our God." Stalin wagged his finger to stop.

"Boys, stop romanticizing. Now let's go join the boys and listen to what the learned teacher has to say. I don't know much about him. I had only arranged a boat ride and lunch at Amrut's house for the boys."

"Stalin, you are fooling us again. You only spoke to us of a boat ride and not of any teacher," protested Caitu

"This talk happened by chance; it was arranged by Marcus and Juju. You just sit there for a while and then we will have lunch and go boating. You had one boat ride already," he snapped as Caitu shook his head mocking his uncle

Cutting short behind the shrine Stalin walked round a boulder and pushed through a bushy fence stepping onto a grassy patch where a group of boys had squatted. Facing them seated under a broad leaved tree were four familiar faces: Kishu, Juju, Marcus and Naique, the GFP man who was seen at the cave. Standing next to Naique was a new face. Though old and frail, his voice had power.

Stalin led Caitu and Bruno to the front row where a lone man among the kids greeted him. Stalin sat down asking the boys to do so. Once seated, their attention turned to the speaker. He made gestures as he spoke:

"Brothers, listen. This beautiful coastal strip was the creation by one of the gods incarnate who was banished on the earth with no land to call his own. He wandered the entire length of the Ghats until he arrived in this region. 'There's no land left for me except the hills above and the sea below. So where can I go?' he said to himself as he sat down exhausted at the foothill 10-12 miles from here. Mind you, this stretch where we are didn't exist then.

Then as he fell into a deep slumber, a voice in the wind alerted him: 'Aren't you a child of god with godly powers? Don't you have powers over the land, sea and the wind? Command them to do what you want them to do'.

When he woke up he had a clear idea of what to do. He commanded the sea: 'Go back far enough so that I have enough land for me,' and the voice in the wind responded to him.

'I will grant you your wish. Shoot an arrow from where you stand as far as you can. And I will give you land that

wide and seven times long.' The godly man shot the arrow as commanded and thus the land was created." The speaker paused as Stalin grumbled to Caitu and put up his hand:

"It is a myth, my friend," he yelled

"Well, my friend that might sound like a mere myth to you. It is written in our books and it has great political and spiritual significance," the teacher responded firmly and added:

"These boys are young and must know their past, be it mythology, culture, history or religion. I have been asked to give a motivational talk. This small coastal stretch is a physical body and a part of Mother India. It cannot remain cut off from the Ghats which are only 40-50 kms away. The gaur and the elephant cross freely in and out of the border but you people here cannot."

As the boys clapped the speaker smiled and folded his hands to them. Stalin now stood up:

"Honored guest! This isn't the time to teach the boys history, religion and mythology. They get enough of it from the gurus, padres or their elders. Our focus must not be just to drive the Portuguese out, but to put the power in the hands of the poor working class. Let's be realistic here. We don't have much time on our hand. Just begin with the real work and strategy and roles that can be assigned to all of us. Let's talk about the plan of action now," he concluded in a firm tone

Taken aback, the teacher stepped aside. Naique got up and folded his hands to him, and then pointed a finger to Stalin:

"Stalin, you have offended our guest, the learned teacher. His account of the sacred origin of this land was meant to educate and inspire these boys here; they need to be inducted in phases. The action plans are for us. There are sets of pamphlets and 20-page booklets, in *Devanagari* and Roman script. The boys will have to digest the contents before they distribute anything to their folks. All the material is in the hut. After lunch we will give it to them," Naique paused and blurted irritably

"Stalin, now that you have already disrupted the teacher's talk you may let the boys leave and have their meals while we deal with our action plan." There was a shout from behind:

"Come on boys. Follow me to the hut. The meals are ready and hot."

"That's Amrut boys; he will take you to the hut for lunch," said Stalin signaling Caitu and Bruno to move

With the boys in tow, Amrut went down a woody trail reaching a row of three huts in a clearing shaded by tall trees.

" Caitu, we have reached a lower point. I am seeing a closer view of the sea below," remarked Bruno. Is this the Amrut's family house?

"You have come to my grandfather's house," said Amrut glancing back

Passing by two huts, Amrut stopped in front of a rectangular hut adjacent to a stone cottage. Outside, a man stood near two steaming pots while another walked up and down inside the hut.

"Bavù! Serve the meals for the boys; they are twelve of them. There will be eight more including myself to follow," said Amrut

"Yes Bavù," the man responded and gave a shout to the man inside the hut, "Lay the plates."

"Boys, go wash your hands and sit down to eat inside," said Amrut clapping his hands

Hand wash done, the boys scrambled inside the hut with a thatched roof and coco-matted walls. At the rear lay a hearth and a table with ladles, spoons, knives and a few utensils.

Banana leaves cut to triple the size of a lunch plate were laid out on the dung floor in two rows two feet apart. Bavù and his helper scooped down steaming hot rice on the leaf-plates followed by a splash of red hot tiger prawn coconut curry. Next to drop on the plates were roasted sardines and a spoonful of pickle. Overpowered by the tangy aroma, the hungry boys bent over to gobble up with gusto.

"It's good for a change; Hindus use *cocum* and tamarind for curry. My mother uses tamarind and vinegar. Have a bellyful Bruno. Season's fresh crop of sardines and tiger prawns it is," enthused Caitu crunching a fat sardine with the bone

The boy opposite Caitu threw a taunt: "You folks eat pork and beef which won't cook without vinegar. And for the feast, you drink and feast like the Portuguese. But you must not eat the mother cow. God will punish you," he yelled grinning

"So what happens when a tiger or jackals eat the cow? Do they get punished?" Caitu taunted back sparking off a hullaballoo attracting Amrut's attention.

"Oi, stop the commotion. No loud chatting whilst eating. The big boys are on their way," he shouted

CHAPTER XII

The Assembly

At the other end the six men assembly was in session. After Stalin's critique of his speech, the teacher walked off towards the temple; then Naique took over. Sitting with Stalin was a guest he had brought along.

By now there was a bit of a gloom and a murmur of gusty wind. Naique looked at the horizon and said:

"Stalin, being a man of action we have accepted you as a part of our organization. Now, since I see a stranger here, you need to introduce him to us. We must hurry before the weather turns nasty."

"He is Ubaldo Fernandes. He runs a printing press in Bombay and has been helping the doctor to print his pamphlets. He is very keen to contribute to our cause. We could use his resources."

"Let him continue his work. Our man will contact him if required," Naique then turned to his colleagues beside him:

"Friends, please go down and sit with our comrade Stalin. It is not right for us to make him a mere part of an audience. We are all one."

The three came down and sat alongside Stalin as Naique resumed:

"Now let's talk of the action plan. August 15 is only weeks away. And my party has vowed to herald a new awakening with bangs, I mean with blasts, if you may call it so. It looks like our people have fallen into a deep slumber. They are hibernating like a frog. But frogs too shake after the thunder and come alive after showers. Well, let me cut short and begin with action plan straight away." He paused to refer to a booklet and resumed:

"The party has decided to put Stalin in charge. Our trainer across the border has certified that he has trained well and has the knowhow to deliver the goods. I mean, we will deliver the goods to him first. Since he is under watch we don't want him to be too visible and arouse suspicion.

Our courier will deliver the material and components to the place he suggests in any of the three villages. We have identified two sites in two South district towns.

Our targets are offices of the Administration and the *Policia Secreta*. One more target will be of Stalin's own choosing. He will assemble, transport and detonate. I am sure Stalin knows to adopt a foolproof camouflage and carry out the plan to the T. The party command has designated Juju and Kishu to assist him. Kishu's assistance is invaluable. Marcus and Juju will also handle propaganda-pamphlet distribution and flag hoisting. So, brothers and comrades, if you approve the plan, please raise your hands."

As three men raised their hands, Stalin put up his hand with a 'V' sign. There was a shout from behind. It was Amrut standing with the teacher.

"Stalin, it is time to move. There's a police jeep going up and down the road. My nephew who lives up there told me they are looking for suspects. Follow me please. We will go to the hut. It is safe there for the time being," said Amrut

As they hurried off Stalin took Amrut aside: "Who are they looking for. Did they give names?"

"Yes indeed; yourself, Kishu, Juju, and importantly one Naique who they said has sneaked through the border. You're putting me in trouble Stalin. You said it was a picnic," Amrut grumbled irritably

"We will not discuss the matter. It happened. Now you have to get the boys out and then us. You are an ace boatman Amrut. We need your help." Stalin's tone was calm.

"Alright, I am moving the boys out first. I will put you all up in my house. You can have your meals there. Bavù will be there with you. I will lock the house from the outside. Stay there till I come back."

Reaching his house Amrut opened the back door and pushed the five men in. It was a small two room house with a kitchen. He asked Bavù and his assistant to take care of them. As Amrut was about to leave, Naique posed a query: "Is this your house Amrut?"

"It is my grandfather's house. I lived here for a while as a kid. Then my father moved out and used this place to build boats. He and a few workers would carve boats out of large tree trunks. They would work at a stretch till the boat was ready. It will be then pulled down into the water. My father is old now. Also, the boats have become narrower for want of tall fat trees. It takes over a century for a tree to grow." Amrut concluded grinning

"Brilliant and admirable work; I salute your father," said Naique grinning back

"Thank you my big Bavù; eat in peace. No one will come here. For your safety, I will lock the house from outside. I will return shortly." Amrut folded his hands and walked down to meet the boys

"Boys, let's go. There's a chance we could encounter a police patrol boat down the stream. Though I can handle them, one never knows," he shouted

"What about the pamphlets?" asked one

"Leave the pamphlets. And listen, I am taking you back by boat. If anyone questions you say we were on a picnic. And furthermore, you have not seen or met anything or anyone. Am I clear?" he retorted

"Amrut, they might ask us questions like what timewe left, where we went and what we ate, for its past lunch time," countered Caitu

"You're clever, nephew of Stalin. We all left at eight in the morning. We trekked up the hill and played over the plateau. Then we ate crackers and cheese which I provided. You paid me three rupias each. You drank water that you brought. Don't ever mention you ate at the hut.

Carry your empty bottles with you. And if they ask if you saw anyone, you saw no one except the crows and the eagles. Remember?"

"Yes!" they all cried in one voice; Amrut was distracted by the blowing wind. He looked up at the gloomy sky and said:

"Now here is something important. When we came in the weather was good. It is getting a bit rough now. I will try and keep the boat as close to the shore line as possible. But should there be an emergency, you will have to jump into the water. I have some inflated tubes and a few banana stems. Grab one each and jump. Those who know to swim may swim ashore. Though I am certain it won't happen, one must be prepared."

Caitu giggled out loud.

"What's so funny Caetano? Is it because you're a good swimmer? Stalin tells me so."

"You are scaring the boys, Amrut. A boatman like you can weather any storm. The weather isn't so bad as yet. It's a bit windy and cloudy. It is raining far out in the sea," snapped Caitu

"You may be a smart talker! Do you know the weather better than me? I am the one who weather the storms out in the sea. You might have done some fishing in the Xapo lake as it dries out. Let's scoot now," Amrut snorted

After locking the back door Amrut set out with the helper as his oarsman. The trail he led the boys was clearer but steeper.

Amrut's boat with a sail was tied to a shrub. After all had climbed in, the helper untied it and jumped in. The two men took to the oars to propel the boat faster. It wobbled under cross currents and wind gusts. It was a lone boat so far out. A few boats were beached on a sand patch or between rocks on the hill side. As the boat approached the narrow strait Amrut's attention was drawn to the long cannon jutting out from a wall on the hillside; two soldiers who stood there sent out signals to Amrut; while one whistled, the other waved a red flag. Before Amrut could wink, a naval motorboat rode in from behind. As the Portuguese officer at the wheel circled round, one of the two armed native police yelled:

"Turn around to the beach and anchor your boat and get down all of you."

Amrut maneuvered the boat as directed and they all got down and waited as the motorboat hovered until it beached into sands. Both the policemen jumped out and confronted Amrut and his helper, asking the boys to move to one side. One of them addressed Amrut in a stern tone: "Where did you come from with these boys?"

"I had taken them for a picnic," he replied

"Strange! A picnic on the hill by the sea in the rains?" the policeman taunted

"Yesterday when the boys came to me, I agreed to take them on my boat; the weather was fine then and also up until now," said Amrut seemingly unsure of himself

The policeman suddenly picked the youngest of the boys who seemed shaken. "Is that true? What time did you all leave in the morning? And what did you do there?"

The boy hesitated for a while only to parrot his own lines: "We all left at eight. We ran around over the plateau; I saw cuckoos and king fisher; also the eagles flew over the sea. Then we ate food."

"What food did you eat?"

"We ate crackers and cheese which he gave us," he said pointing to Amrut, and, "we paid him three rupias each for the trip," uttered the boy
"A very truthful boy." Then he turned to Amrut:

"Did you meet or see any men there? Stalin, Juju, and other bandits who were seen moving about?"

"I know Stalin but I didn't see him or anyone else," said Amrut, a bit confidently

By now the Portuguese officer had got off his boat and was inside Amrut's boat doing a search. When he appeared on the scene Amrut greeted him with folded hands. The officer gave him a nod and spoke to the policeman. The policeman noted down the boys' names, and their details. Then he addressed Amrut in a firm tone:

"In the first place, it is an offence to take these boys out at sea in your boat. Your boat is for catching fish and not to cruise. Secondly, it is dangerous to be out in this weather in such a boat with no proper safety devices. My officer tells me you had just three tire tubes and stems of banana plant. Did you think you're going for a swim in a rivulet? You've risked the life of these boys. This should not happen again. The officer has pardoned you this time. Go now and reach the boys safely home."

"I thank the officer. Please allow me to offer him a large king fish, the finest of the morning catch with no scratch. I will be at the wharf. Let someone collect it," said Amrut and folded his hands looking towards the officer who gave him an inscrutable grin.

Amrut was in an elated spirit and despite the gusty wind and watery whorls, the boat ploughed into the river mouth and headed upstream amid a hullabaloo of yells and laughter of the boys as Caitu having put the inflated tube round his neck, mimed a mock rehearsal, almost jumping overboard. Amrut was furious:

"Stalin's nephew, are you mad? Put that tube where it was. If you slip and fall, I won't be able to save you," he yelled

"I can swim a mile Amrut," he snapped as he got off the prow edge and put the tube down

"Oh really? There are undercurrents and cross currents. Anyway, I will have no more picnics and outings on my boat for you or Stalin. If not for my good relationship with the officer, I would have been nabbed today. Stalin had told me it was a picnic for the boys and teachers. But as I stood there I heard them speak of planting bombs. He trapped me," cried Amrut

At the wharf Amrut dismissed them all in haste. Caitu cycled back home at speed under a drizzle. He kept mum as Bruno kept chiding him till he reached home. Bruno quickly changed into his clothes and walked away with his umbrella, visibly disturbed. Caitu followed him begging him to get on his bicycle. After a bit of a fuss, Bruno agreed and asked Caitu to drop him near the neighboring village, the way he had come. Then he walked back home.

CHAPTER XIII

The die is cast

It was five in the afternoon. Matilda and the neighbor girl were seated in verandah and Ana was standing at the door.

Matilda alias Matil of 25 years had built a reputation as a woman of great resource that the villagers and womenfolk in particular had begun to rely on. Though she was an inquisitive busybody, people did not mind it because she rarely did anything hurtful or nasty. She never pitted one against the other and intervened where the cause was just. She was Ana's close friend.

"The ward boys had come for you saying there's a game. But you look worn out Bruno," said his mother as Bruno came up

"Bruno, what's so special about this new friend Caetano that got you so attached to?" remarked Matil

"Caetano is my new classmate and he needs help in his studies. He is a fine footballer, swimmer, plays banjo and sings. Didn't you hear of the little girl who died after their doctor's wrong diagnosis a year ago? That was his sister Matil," said Bruno

"Oh yes, it was a rare outbreak of diphtheria that the doctor didn't even suspect. Being the first victim she alerted and saved three children who were treated in time. Whose son is this Caetano?

"He is Caetano Silva; his mother's name is Marta; his uncle Santolino Silva is a freedom fighter."

"Oh you mean Stalin? They say he is a communist. You must keep away from them Bruno," she retorted

"I have nothing to do with his uncle. I went to see him as he wasn't well. Now I am off for the game." Bruno rushed into the house.

He came back after a few minutes wearing boots and sprinted off under a light drizzle. The outlying fields being under monsoon siege, a sandy patch by the Cross at the field's edge came in handy to enliven the boys' dampened spirits. The summer vacationers having gone, there were fewer players. When Bruno reached there, two patched up teams of six and seven were in action. One of the players yelled from the playground:

"Upper Ward boy, get into our team."

They're one player short," said a balding man standing under an umbrella by the Cross. A seaman on vacation, he was a stand-alone referee.

Upper Ward was playing against Lower Ward. With Bruno joining his team, they were seven to a side. Despite the drizzle and stoppages due to disputes of rough play, off-sides, and complaints against refereeing, the game went on until it was too dark to spot the ball.

The match ended when the Upper Ward goalkeeper got knocked on the head by an unsighted ball.

The referee gave away the kitty for the winning team though the disputes stayed on as the boys and men dispersed in twos and threes towards their homes.

Going home Bruno had a warm bath that his mother had kept ready for him. He was a bit unnerved seeing her quiet and distant. He felt it as he entered; she didn't pester him with her queries as was her habit. She only spoke a few words and walked into her bedroom. She had not lit the lamp on. Standing at the doorway, Bruno spoke into her darkened room:

"Mãe! Shall we eat? I am quite hungry."

She came out into the passage where a lamp lay burning on a table below the little altar.

"You forgot about the prayer Bruno. Let's pray the rosary." Her tone was firm.

They prayed the rosary and she laid out the supper for both of them. She ate quietly which again Bruno found strange.

"Something worrying you mãe? Is father not well?" he asked

"Your father is fine. But what is worrying me is that you're going to Belgaum in a week's time. You're going to stay with aunt Aurelia. She arrived yesterday and dropped in this morning. She said your father said it is final. He's written a letter to me but I haven't received it yet," she said grumpily

Bruno looked at her with mouth agape.

"What happened mãe? How this sudden decision when father isn't even here? How did he do that? Also, it's over a month now schools have started. I had thought of helping out my friend in his studies."

"Oh you mean Caetano? He is a big strong boy and talks big. Do you think he needs your help? And don't you know he is the reason that you are being sent away?" she whined

"Strong in body but weak in the head mãe and also kind at heart; I've learned him well. He needs help," Bruno persisted

"So you learnt him well and think you can tutor him. But I am still learning you. Things have been happening and you haven't told me anything.

But your father knows more than you and me. He has a few close friends who could have seen you; the professor for example. Aurelia's husband is from Velem. He has his relatives and friends. I sensed it after she told me a few things. I had always opposed your father to take you away from home. But now that it's done, I will not object to it." She seemed more composed now:

"Are you ready for it Bruno?" she asked abruptly

Bruno looked into her eyes; they were moist.

"I am ready if you are mãe. After all it isn't far; here to Londa and then to Belgaum by rail or by bus through the Ghats, though most people prefer to travel by rail. But I wouldn't miss an opportunity to come home even if it is for a couple of days." Bruno tried to comfort her.

"But that might come to an end. There are rumors." Ana was curt again.

"Oh! Did Matilda tell you that mother? Her brother works as a forest guard. She will tell the whole world if she knows anything," he grumbled

"Matilda didn't tell me that. Your aunt did. You know Aurelia's husband works as a clerk at the military base. She talked of some moves but didn't say more. She has to be careful too. Why do you always belittle Matilda behind her back?" Ana frowned at her son

"Sorry mãe. I know Matil is an intelligent girl. She is your bosom friend too."

"Ummhum; She is, the one and only. My son is smart too." She leaped up to him pinching his cheek.

"So mãe, how do I proceed if I have to leave immediately? I have to get a passport first and then…. Oh! I don't know anything about processing the travel papers."

"Don't worry. Aurelia is coming here tomorrow morning. She's been in and out of the territory and knows the formalities. Her daughter Maureen got married and is in Bombay. You can either stay with aunt or join the school boarding. She said to keep your school and birth certificates ready. She will come with a taxi to take you to places you need to go. Good for you my son," she said with relief

"Oh really, that is nice of her. What all places we will visit; certainly we will be going to town."

"Of course, you'll be going to town because that's where you do the passports. I don't know what all places she will take you too. Your father hasn't taken me out much," she said in an accusatory tone

As they chatted Bruno began to doze and his mother told him to go to sleep.

"I will sleep in your room tonight. Lay a mat for me," he mumbled

"I will," she said fondly

By 8:30 next morning aunt Aurelia was at their door. The handsome middle-aged woman was Bruno's father's cousin sister who had married to David from Velem, who had worked as a clerk at the British army camp at Belgaum. With the departure of the British, he was absorbed by the Indian army.

Bruno had just returned from the chapel after serving the first mass.

"Good morning Bruno, are you ready with the two certificates?" Aurelia chirped walking energetically up and down despite her plump figure. She hugged him nearly choking him.

"Of course auntie" said the boy, a little out of breath as his mother watched on

"I have laid breakfast for you Aurelia, omelet and coffee," said Ana

"Breakfast I already had. I will have the coffee as Bruno gets ready to leave," she said as she plopped down on the arm chair at the entrance, flattening the plump pillow underneath. Bruno came out after breakfast followed by his mother.

"We have to go to a couple of places first, the vicar and then the police station at Kunkali," said Aurelia getting up from the armchair

"Police station auntie, for what?" said Bruno with alarm in his voice

"Are you scared? Why?" she asked with a skewed smile

Bruno glanced at his mother and said: "Not scared auntie; now, give me a few minutes. I will go and get my things; they are in my mother's cupboard."

"I have put them in your school bag Bruno inside a magazine; birth certificate, two originals, school mark sheet, one. Keep your bag safe from rain," said his mother

After glugging her coffee, Aurelia got up to speak:

"Oh, a mark-sheet isn't the only thing; we also need the character certificate and then his school has to translate it into Portuguese. But don't you worry, I got it done. We only need to collect it from the office. I went to the principal's house and told him that Bruno is leaving; *'Why are you taking away our good student and which school will admit him so late?' he said to me disappointedly*

"So everything is done, Aurelia. So nice of you," said Ana with a wide smile

"Not at all, it's just the beginning. After collecting the report from his school, we run to catch the vicar. That's just a stone-throw away from there. You know, vicar's letter carries weight. But I don't know your vicar and he may not know Bruno; so we first go to the chaplain who will surely write a good word about Bruno. Well, letters from the vicar or the chaplain carry weight with the government officials," Aurelia blurted out pacing up and down. Then she sat down again.

"You're so clever Aurelia. You may also know the principal at the English school. Your daughter had studied for two years there," said Ana

"That principal is long gone, Ana. He was only a matriculate but a dedicated man. The school remained closed for a while. There was no Christ monument then, just an open ground right up to the church. Then the school was re-opened by a graduate." As Aurelia plumped down again Bruno turned up with a bag over his shoulder.

"Let's go auntie Aurelia," said the boy

"Oh yes, the taxi man might run away. I left him by the chapel," she said and got up from the chair

The chaplain was extremely disappointed and kept asking Aurelia why this sudden rush when school year had already started. Aurelia who didn't want to argue or explain merely said it was his father's decision.

Beginning from the chapel to the school and finally at the church the jobs got done with so much ease that made Bruno look up at Aurelia with awe. An hour later at ten they left the precincts of the Osnem church and the taxi headed to Kunkali. Bruno got nervy as the taxi passed by the church reaching the junction.

"I am not coming in there. The inspector had seen me with Caetano near the cave. They let me off but took away Caetano for questioning. We had gone on a picnic. You're so influential auntie. Just take my papers and do the needful. Will you please, aunt Aurelia?" His voice quavered.

They were seated on the back seat. Seeing the boy alarmed she beamed a wide smile:

"So what if he has seen you. You haven't done a crime?"

The taxi driver turned round briefly: "I will tell you once we're out of the taxi," said Bruno as Aurelia turned to the driver:

"You may park your vehicle by the Cross here. It's only a minute walk for us,"

"I will wait here. They don't allow taxis to wait near the police station," the driver responded

They got out of the taxi and Bruno told his aunt briefly of what happened at the cave. She turned serious and then laughed away.

"You come with me Bruno. I will handle everything. Just hold the umbrella over us. It's drizzling." With her arm around his shoulder she led him to the cottage that housed the Kunkali outpost. After a few minutes wait they were called in.

Gushing out honey-mouthed greetings, a beaming Aurelia walked to the inspector's table. He got up and offered his hand and asked her and the boy to sit. He looked the boy over again.

"I have seen this boy somewhere," he said sternly

"Have you Inspector? He is quite a shy and yet an adventurous boy; he likes wandering around the villages. You might have seen him near Pandava cave with his schoolmate Caetano who took him there on a picnic," she asserted keeping Bruno on the edge

"Oh the nephew of Stalin; he is a strong, intelligent and yet a stupid boy. His mother says he is affected by some trauma. A few years ago he was caught with GFP propaganda leaflets. He told us he had picked the bundle from the road side. And this last summer I had accompanied the *Agente* of *Polícia Secreta*. He had a tip off that a GFP senior was at the cave with local supporters. But they fled. We found this boy and that Caetano loitering there. We took away Caetano for questioning about Stalin but couldn't get anything out from him. We let him off after his mother turned up." The inspector broke off to refer to his diary and resumed:

"Yesterday I got a call from the naval police that suspects were spotted at Betul hill top. I sent my junior and a constable to follow up. The suspects fled again. But a naval boat chased a fishing boat with a group of boys who were seen at the hill top. The boatman told the police they had gone on a picnic. Strange indeed, whenever activists have their meetings boys go on a picnic." The inspector chuckled and added:

"We treat our youth humanely knowing they are being used by the hard core elements as a cover. Now tell me Aurelia what brings you here with this boy."

Aurelia spoke after a hesitation: "Inspector, the boy is the son of my cousin brother who wants to shift him to a Belgaum school for his remaining two years. So I have come for a 'No Objection letter' to apply for his travel document."

The inspector gave the boy a long hard look. He sniggered and then asked for his documents. He mumbled as he skimmed through the letters:

"Doing daily service at the chapel, studying well and bears an excellent character at the chapel, school.... Aha.....and yet keeping company of a boy with the worst record at school?"

He frowned as he spoke:

"Though your character certificates and school reports are excellent, you are keeping company with a trouble-maker. This calls for further investigation before we issue a clearance. Boy, with all your intelligence and cool you're unable to help yourself."

As Aurelia kept pleading with him, the inspector remained unresponsive. Then he gave the boy a hard look again, shook his head and blurted:

"Well, I shall help you out this time. It is better you go away before you get into real trouble. I will give you the police clearance. But try to learn lessons from your stupid mistakes. You may find your lessons at school easy but lessons of life are tougher. Do you hear me?" he concluded in a stern tone wagging a finger as Bruno mumbled: 'yes sir'

Then he called his assistant and instructed him to do the needful.

"You may sit in the verandah till the clearance report is done," concluded the inspector offering Aurelia a hand. Bruno got up, still a bit tense. Aurelia thanked the inspector showering him with a few more parting honey phrases and walked away pulling Bruno along. They got back into the taxi and headed to the district town.

At six in the evening Aurelia dropped Bruno at the end of the bund road and he made a run amid a shower and reached home.

"Have a wash Bruno. I will serve you some tea and biscuits," said his mother

"I had a bellyful at *Pençao Royal* hotel and then the German ice-cream at the Penguin; but there was no German there."

"He was stranded here during the war and left after the war ended. Now it is run by a local. Tell me, when will get your passport," she asked

"It might take a week. But mother, the passport agent took away all my certificates. Aunt told me to get four copies each from school and the church. She also asked me to check with the Passport Agent to make sure everything was in order. She said she is very busy with her house work for the next few days. That means I have to miss classes for the next two days, with permission of course. It is her suggestion." Bruno chuckled seemingly content.

"She knows what she is doing. She is in charge of you now. Aurelia is an angel. She cares about you as much as I do. But now I will be alone and sad when you're gone. Since the arrival of Aurelia, I've been thinking just what made your father to take this drastic step. And how could he do it barely over a month after he had begun his voyage. His letter arrived this afternoon, a part of which is addressed to you. He said you had fallen into bad company and he feared you might land up in jail. So on his way to Bombay he dropped at Aurelia's place and begged her and her husband to find you a school and to keep you with them until matriculation. They told him they would be happy to keep you, as their daughter had moved to Bombay with her husband. Anyway, now that you've agreed I will not speak any more about it. You can read your part of the letter."

Her son protested:

"But mãe, I wonder just how he knew where and with whom I move about. Or what bad company I have. Caetano is not a loafer or a rowdy boy."

"He might not be a bad boy at heart. But he gets into fights and uses foul language. I heard it myself. That makes him rowdy. You cannot give excuses for him. Caetano is also under police watch because of his uncle."

"How do you know he picks up fights?" Bruno asked

"Didn't he beat up someone at the church? Professor then warned you to stay away from him. Then you two went for a picnic at the Pandava cave and were caught by the police. You never told me about it. I had suspected something the day Caetano came home. I overheard him and you said it's nothing. And don't you know Professor gets all the information from the inspector? He has surely told your father and also written to him. Also, Aurelia's in-laws from Velem might have seen you with Caetano and informed her. Who knows?" she moaned

As tasked by his aunt, Bruno got his jobs done in the next two days, setting aside the afternoons to visit his close relatives in and around the three villages. The day he was to resume school he got delayed at the chapel as he had to hand over the charge.

Nearing his class he tried to rush in through the door but the teacher stopped him:

"Bruno, you missed a class. And we heard you're leaving. What happened suddenly? You were doing fine here."

"It is my father's decision," said Bruno

The teacher exited after asking him to take his seat. Bruno moved to his bench and sat next to Caitu who seemed unusually quiet. He smiled faintly when Bruno greeted him. As Bruno sat down the boys posed queries: "Are you really leaving Bruno? When? And why now in the middle of school?"

Bruno brushed off the pleas saying: "Not yet finalized."

The geography teacher came in, and holding a textbook in his hand he began:

"Let's follow up from where we left off last. Our subject was the wild life in the prairies, grasslands and semi-arid river valleys of North America. We know that the prominent animal in this region is the bison."

The teacher walked to the drawing board, drew two sketches and turned round:

"Look at the sketches that are also there in your text book. It is the bison of North America but a similar animal is also found in the Savannas of South America and Africa and even in India. Do you find this animal familiar?" he asked as a boy stood up to answer:

"Yes sir. My family moved in here years ago from the north east of this territory where we have similar animal. We call it *the gaur*. The bison of America you have drawn has hair on the head and its legs and also a big hump on the back. Our gaur is hairless and has large curved horns. But the gaurs used to trouble us by entering our villages and eating or destroying our crops. Sometimes they would stand in our path; though they didn't mean to attack us, but one could never tell. When our elders reported to the regidor or police, they would ask them to shoot the gaur with the gun. But our elders refused to kill the gaur because it is the relative of the cow. They wanted the government to do that." The teacher asked the boy to stop and to sit down

"Gaur is an animal. Your crop might be your food; it is also the animal's food. Also, you have strayed from our subject. Our subject is geography. The bison in India or in Africa is called a buffalo. Our region doesn't have large grassland plains."

The teacher stopped seeing the school peon at the door. He shuffled in and handed the teacher a note. After reading it he called out:

"Caetano, pick up your bag and go to the office now."

The boy walked out showing no reaction except a glance at Bruno. Later the news was out that the police had taken him away for questioning.

The next few days Caitu did not attend the class. Not just his class but other classes too were always curious to know about Caitu. The boy was both loved and hated by students and teachers alike. Egged on by the bold and inquisitive boys, the peon spilled the beans: *Caetano's mother had visited the office and informed the principal that Caetano had gone away to see his ailing grandma and so would not be attending school for a week or more.*

After another week, Bruno's travel documents arrived. Aurelia decided that they leave for Belgaum after two days. A day before he was to leave he went to Caitu's house. Meeting his mama, he told her he was going away and the reason behind it.

"So I came to bid good-bye to you both," said Bruno

"Caetano has gone away with his uncle, my brother," said Marta with a sad face

"Where is his uncle's house? Can I go and see him there?" Bruno asked

"It is also my house where I had lived until I got married. It is very far from here, in the foothills of the Ghats. There are woods, springs and caves. Caetano would take you there one day. But he would feel terrible knowing that you have gone away. For the first time I've seen him so attached to a calm and quiet boy. Anyway, I wish you all the best and pray that all your dreams come true." Her tone had an emotional ring.

When he was about to leave, she smiled and gave him a tight hug and pecks on the cheeks.

CHAPTER XIV

Bruno's last night at home

The night before he was to depart Bruno asked his mother to sleep in his room. After she had spread the two mats Bruno went down to sleep. And they chatted.

"It is the first time you're travelling by train Bruno. I have only travelled from our district town to the port town to see your father when the ship touched there. But you will be crossing the Ghats and watch Dudh Sagar waterfall. They say the train passes by 'the sea of milk', so close that you can hold out your hand and scoop some of it.

And when you reach Belgaum, I don't know how you're going to take it. Your father says the climate is very good. And they have lights and fans there."

"And there is cinema and also the big circus mãe," enthused the boy

"So it means you will soon forget your mother Bruno! Promise you will write to me at least twice a month."

"I will write every week to my mother. I promise. Don't you worry about it? And didn't I tell you I will come home at every opportunity I get? I wonder how those schools are though I heard they're far more superior. That's understandable. We don't have too many English schools here."

"Aurelia has been always boasting about two schools in Belgaum: St. Pauls for the boys and St. Joseph's convent for the girls where her daughter studied. She said if you don't get in as a boarder you will have to cycle your way from their house."

"I prefer cycling to school mãe."

"I will be missing you Bruno, Oh how I will take it Bruno. I will miss you so much!" she exclaimed and suddenly caught him tight and he held on to her.

"It's the first time you caught me so tight mãe. I don't remember when you hugged me like that. It felt so nice. You know Caetano's mama hugged me a couple of times like that," he mumbled

Ana let go of her hands and pushed him away in a huff: "Oh, so you felt it was her who caught you, that step-mother of yours? I hate you," she cried

"No mãe, never! And she is not my step-mother. I have only one mother, you are my one and only mãe," he whimpered as he caught her. Now give me another hug like that and sing me a lullaby that you used to sing for me when I was a baby. I only remember my grandma's little songs because I used to sleep with her most of the time," said Bruno.

She gave him a tighter hug and the boy sighed.

"Strange Bruno; I used to hold you and sing for you till you were four. Can't you remember anything at all? What a shame?" she said and started singing tapping at his back

"I can see that you're falling off to sleep. May be I am boring you," she murmured but he didn't answer

She stopped when he started to snore softly.

CHAPTER XV

Bruno leaves by the West of India Portuguese Guaranteed Railway

The next morning Bruno arrived at the railway station accompanied by his mother and Matilda. A solitary roofed platform overlooked two meter-gauge rail tracks. Midway of the platform was the unmanned gate, the only point of entry or exit for the passengers. Beside it in a small room a man seated across a table was both the station master and the ticketing clerk.

A man in khaki uniform tried to enter the cabin. A shout from the clerk made him scurry across the platform and ring the bell, a frantic and repetitive ring. A minute later a steaming railway engine whistled in tugging half a dozen coaches. The train had come in from the port town.

Amidst a scramble of a sort, Aurelia pulled Bruno along and got into a coach and grabbed the two window seats on one side. The bags were put in place with Matilda's able assistance. Ana and Matilda hung on there until it was time for them to leave. A tearful and emotional hug from his mother made Bruno tearful too.

Ana and Matilda watched from the platform as the train rolled out under a drizzle. The coal-fired engine at the front chuffed on billowing black fumes, whistling every few minutes; it seemed to say: *'I am coming, stay away from the tracks.'*

It wended its way across a dense rural setting bypassing manned level crossings where pedestrians of the divided village stood on either side, under umbrellas or in raincoats; a few stood holding on to their bicycles.

The rustic folks looked up in amazement at the muscular fireman in a dirty boiler suit hauling coal into the red burning cauldron as the steam locomotive chugged along heading to the hills. Even as the rattle and the whistles died off, the echoes lingered in their ears.

The train's first stop was a brief one at a quiet single-platform station. Half an hour on, the train halted at a busier station; at one side of its perimeter was a yard with dumps of ore and trucks on the outside. A few passengers got off the train and a few more climbed in among them an elderly couple. The woman sat near Aurelia and her husband pushed in beside Bruno.

Thereafter the train moved into a more wooded terrain with houses sparse or non-existent. After three quarters of an hour of a gradual climb of the first foothill of the Ghats, the train stopped at Colem. The station served as the Portuguese immigration check-post, though it wasn't the last of the territory. Passengers scrambled onto the platform with only hand bags or shoulder bags.

"Pick up the shoulder bag Bruno. We are going for an immigration check," said Aurelia

"How far and how long will it take? Are we leaving our suitcases here?" asked Bruno

"They are sitting out there on the platform. We get through quicker here than on the Indian side as we have no customs-check like they have at Castle Rock. And don't worry about the suitcases. Nobody will touch our bags. Further on we need to be careful though," she said

The elderly couple got down and joined them, but half way down the man mumbled into his wife's ear and headed for the bar.

"Oh these men they are going for their last gulp of scotch or a glass of beer. In Bombay they would have to go back to bootlegger's hooch," the woman grumbled limping behind Aurelia who responded with a chuckle

A bit of a crowd had queued up at the Immigration desk. One Portuguese and two native assistants manned a longish table while two armed guards watched over. The Portuguese officer gave Bruno a long suspicious look as he scrutinized his document making him tense. He exchanged a word with the native assistant who turned to Aurelia:

"What is the reason for the boy to leave in a hurry? This passport is just a few days old. Is he not attending school?"

"Senhor, the boy's father wants to send him to Africa; so he is joining St. Paul's, an English school in Belgaum. We don't have a good English school in the village."

"Oh really?" said the assistant as he translated Aurelia's explanation to the Portuguese officer

The officer grinned at Aurelia and then greeted his senior who stood a few yards away with a pint of St. Pauli beer. The two Portuguese guffawed; the senior seemed annoyed at the assistant as he moved out of sight. The assistant kept Bruno's passport aside making Aurelia and the boy tense.

The senior reappeared at the table, glanced at Bruno and then looked into his passport and threw it back to the assistant and gave a nod to stamp the exit.

With great relief Aurelia and Bruno hurried back to their compartment. As they sat to have their snacks and refreshments, their carriage began to jerk amid loud knocks and steam whistles.

"What's happening to the train auntie; these knocks, hisses and jerks?" Bruno asked munching a patty

"They're adding an engine at the back to power the train to climb the Ghats," said Aurelia

"Um, good brains," quipped Bruno

"Yes indeed, of the British, not the Portuguese, butthey are gone now," she chuckled giving him a pat

From Colem the train made a steady run through a thicker forest. Bruno peeped through a half-shut window. In the backdrop of a hill range under shower he watched the train climb, at times slanting to one side; of a sudden it entered a tunnel engulfing all into darkness, but only for a minute.

Exiting the tunnel it passed along a decrepit platform with a signboard 'Sonaulim' on one side and a side track on the other. A wider hill range loomed in and out of sight due to the tall forest trees along the track.

Aurelia alerted the boy:

"Bruno, keep watching as the train goes round the Ghats. It will circle round the hills a few times giving you a distant and then closer view of the waterfall; finally, it will fly pass by it."

With his eyes glued to the hills, Bruno got the first glimpse of the fall; four milky veins across the dark green canvas of the hill. The train circled round and he saw it again. He pointed it to Aurelia:

"Is that the waterfall auntie? But it is still away and the train is only rounding and rounding."

As she leaned to look out the train flew past it and soon shot into darkness again accompanied by a resounding rattle. When it emerged from the tunnel the hills to the right appeared closer. Aurelia turned to Bruno:

"Sorry, I missed that snapshot. Listen, the train seems to be going in circles but it's pushing up and on through the Ghats. I don't know how they built these circular tracks. It must have been tough."

The old man beside Bruno broke in:

"Listen boy! I will tell you how they built this railway; there was this wide range of rolling hills to cross through to reach a higher elevation on the east of the Ghats.

As a rail road requires a stable surface on low hills, they had to make over a dozen tunnels through hills and link the gaps or gorges between them with a dozen bridges and viaducts. I heard the surveyors got leads from the shepherds and goatherds who over generations had trekked the Ghats on either side." The man paused to cough and added:

"You shall now get the final view of the waterfall but there are a couple of tunnels to pass through. So keep looking."

"Thank you uncle," said Bruno. With many regular commuters like the old man or Aurelia, the first time passengers got pre-alerted.

The boy saw the same milky veins, fuller and closer, spilling down the murky green hill; wooly clouds loomed overhead blanketing the somber monsoon sky; the valleys below receded deeper under a canopy of green.

Then as the man had said, the train sneaked in and out through two short tunnels and ran over the viaduct. The *Dhud Sagar*, the 'sea of milk', bloated by the monsoons gushed down the rugged darkened rocks spraying droplets right up to the window. Bruno thrust his hand out and caught some of it. As the train trundled down the bridge the roaring waters, backed by the dak-tak-dak-tak rattle-rhythm, echoed across the hills.

"Where is the Dudh Sagar station uncle?" asked Bruno

"It should come after one more tunnel. But you might not find anybody there, may be a guard," he said

After tunnel five, the train halted at a narrow platform. It was the Dudh Sagar station. One Portuguese and a native with a rifle jumped in from left end.

"Does anybody live around here?" asked the boy

"The villages are in the valley down on the other side. It's easier for them to come up here and hop on the train; down there they have to walk miles to reach the road to the nearest town. Now there isn't much we can see from this end except the forest trees and rocks. Let's go to the other side to get a better view. The man by the window is dozing. I shall request him to move a little or take our seat. People are obliging here," said the old man grinning at Bruno

The man who was dozing obliged as was anticipated. The view below was exquisite, an expanse of beautiful green valley encircled by low rolling hills.

"I can see a cottage and a temple hidden down there. Oh that's where the village is. Still, how lonely it must be?" said Bruno

"There are few scattered hamlets, each with a dozen or more households in that forest. Soon, we will reach, Caranzol, our last station."

"Oh I heard of Caranzol but I've never met anyone from that village," said Bruno

The old man gave him a toothy grin: "I once met a man at Colem who had come to buy liquor. He had hopped on the train from the Caranzol's platform. He told me in the village a few dozen families live a healthy and happy life drinking spring water and eating fresh vegetables. A few of them eat the wild boar."

At Caranzol the train made a brief halt letting the Portuguese officer and the native guard jump off on to the platform.

"Bruno, the train will now make its final steep ascent giving you a beautiful close view of the upper range of hills as it goes past the last stretch of 6-7 kms. But there are still five more tunnels before we reach Castle Rock. This is the last tract of the 26 km trail from Colem that the Portuguese called the Braganza Ghats. I don't know why they called that; may be some Braganza had finalized the WIPGR project," said the man as Bruno responded:

"No uncle! Our Portuguese professor had told us the name originated from the House of Braganza founded in 1412 in the northern Bragança district of Portugal. The imposing castle with a tower on a hill played a military and defensive role against the warring kingdoms of Leon and Castile until 1580 when King Philip of Spain united Portugal with Spain. When that ended around 1640 until the end of 19th century this royal house gave Portugal its dukes, governors, kings and even emperors." As Aurelia a few elders listened keenly, Bruno paused as if to recall something and then resumed:

"But there is another parallel here. Around the time this railway was built, Portugal built its meter gauge Tua railway joining that remote Bragança district to Porto. That railway runs through the scenic valley of Tua river. It was also built over rugged terrain. Is it not then similar to our own that joins Mormugão port to Castle Rock railway and then to India?" Bruno concluded with a question

Aunt Aurelia leaned over to give him a hug and the old man gave him a pat:

"Bruno, you are a wise head on your young shoulders; now you gave us a history lesson," he chuckled

From Caranzol, after a relentless climb with numerous sharp turns and crossing the five tunnels including the longest of over 400 meters, the train moved on the high plateau of Castle Rock where the passengers were put to a strenuous test. While the customs did a thorough check of the bags, immigration officials scrutinized every document, and having confirmed that every traveler was a bona fide Portuguese subject, the passports were stamped.

After another half hour the train whistled passed a hillock and entered the Londa Junction. From the platform the raucous yells of "chai, chai" rang out. Tea- boys with tea-pots and baby glasses in metal holders jumped into the compartments; a few of them served the passengers from the platform pushing glasses through barred windows. Aurelia and Bruno had a few more snacks. During the long halt, the train began to move up and down and there was the same banging and puffing as it did at Colem.

"Now what are they doing to the train auntie? There's no more climb. Are they taking off the extra engine or what? Oh so funny!" exclaimed Bruno

"Funny indeed! At Colem they added an extra engine; now they're adding more coaches to make the train twice long. It would now become a 14-hour Londa-Miraj- Poona Mail. It would take in more passengers stopping at stations along the way until Poona. But for us it is just a 3-hour journey to Belgaum," she uttered

At last the train whistled off the way it had come in.

"Oh! What's this auntie? The long train is going backwards, the same way we came. Are we going back to Goa?"

"Bruno, just keep looking ahead, "she smirked

The train headed towards the hillock it had come by, but as it neared it, it turned to its right trundling onto another track.

Aurelia sniggered watching Bruno's face.

"I got it; it's not going the same way." He grinned at her.

"We've crossed the Ghats and the train is on its way to Belgaum by the Southern Mahratta Railway," she beamed

CHAPTER XVI

A brief reunion

During his two academic years of 1951-54 in Belgaum, Bruno came home thrice. On his very first Christmas home-coming in 1951 he kept away from Caetano as his father was down. During the 1952 summer visit he bumped into his pal in the bazaar. Overjoyed, Caitu coaxed him to come home. Marta greeted Bruno as he came up the steps and escorted him into the side room.

A re-look at the photos rekindled Bruno's memory of not long ago. A larger retouched picture of Ann Marie hung on the wall above the showcase. Marta made Bruno to sit on the settee and plumped beside him. With an arm round his shoulder she enquired about his health, family and school. As they lay immersed as if in a mother-and-child reunion, Caitu showed up with his banjo. Pulling a chair, he sat down and played a couple of songs as the two watched and listened. Then as Marta excused herself and left, Caitu put aside the banjo and took her place. Bruno shot a barrage of questions:

"Caitu, you play well and seem more relaxed. Now tell me how you're doing at school, and more importantly, why you were called to the office that day? And what made you flee to the hills? Also, have you stopped drinking?"

"So many queries, Bruno! Well I made it to Class VI with difficulty; don't know if I would finish my matric. Papa is upset as usual; he left a month ago. I play the banjo more regularly now and might even join a band. A band boy taught me many new songs. I find it easier to learn songs than lessons Bruno," he sniggered and added:

"My drinking is more controlled. I am a social drinker now, a few times in a month. I play a bit less of football."

"Playing banjo or joining a band is fine Caitu, but your controlled social drinking worries me. I've heard these excuses from addicts. You say you play less of football too. And why should you drink at all? You're still a school boy," Bruno retorted irritably

"Not to worry! I am at peace now. About my fleeing to the hills, remember the police had noted down our names at the Little Finger beach; so, as a precaution I stayed at my cousin's. Not finding me at home, the police came to the school; that's the day I was called to the office, remember? They took me to the outpost and questioned me about Stalin, and the picnic on the hilltop. Even as Cipriano whipped my palm, I stuck to the truth as I saw it."

"What did you tell them?" asked Bruno

About Stalin, mama was my guide and inspiration and about the picnic and the boat ride, it was Amrut, the boatman and the little boy," Caitu sniggered.

"Little boy is a little boy. You are a big boy and need to be more truthful to yourself," quipped Bruno, "and then you left for the foothills?"

"Yes, the same afternoon mama's brother, Alexandre came home in a jeep. I hadn't seen him for years. He took me to my mama's home. It lies in a remote hamlet by a side river. A glance at the river gave me a flashback: I remembered walking over a shaky palm-bridge with mama holding my hand. I must have been a five year old then."

"You are a story teller Caitu. So you walked the same palm bridge with Alexandre?" asked Bruno

"Oh no, Alexandre made me cross a brand new iron bridge. But it was a long way off. Crossing it we reached Baga village and then went down a long winding forest path, forded a stream, walked over a smaller palm bridge to reach Alexandre's house."

"Oh there is another Baga village there? Anyway, it must have been a nice hideout for you away from temptations. How long did you stay there?" asked Bruno

"Only for a day as Alexandre put me up with his uncle Simplicio in the main village. I felt better, as granny kept grumbling about this and that. Simplicio showed me around the caves and the springs. One evening he took me to a pub but gave me only a lime-soda. The pub seemed to be the only place alive in the bazaar nook. Finding me curious about the caves, a man told me a few things. He said a hermit who has cures for all human ailments visits the cave and that a few have been lucky to meet him and got cured of their illness or woes." Astonished, Bruno broke in:

"You should have stayed and met the hermit then."

"How could I hang on in the jungle till I met him?" He sniggered and walked to the gramophone and spun a record.

"I will be back in an instant Bruno," he said and hurried out of the room. He came back sooner with two bottles of St. Pauli beer.

"What's this? I am not drinking," Bruno protested

"I missed you at school. I saw you during last Christmas but stayed away as you were with your father. Now, I would have surely done better had you stayed back. I am happy you came over. Just have one glass of beer Bruno to share my joy. You will be gone soon," Caitu pleaded

"Alright, one glass, but I have a request. I'm coming down this Christmas with aunt Aurelia and her husband David. Their daughter Maureen who is a good singer would be joining us if her husband is on duty; he is a junior officer in the Navy. Aunt and Maureen will be with us for four days till Christmas Eve. On Christmas day they will go to David's house. I told you where my aunt is married. The reason I am telling you because I want you to accompany our carol singers on the banjo and give good rhythm. Our village is expecting families from Bombay and Africa. Prof. Leitão who is an ace violinist would be happy to hear you play. Keep yourself free for us Caitu. It will be my last Christmas together before I finish school and move out to Bombay," Bruno enthused with a sparkle in his eyes

" I envy you Bruno. You can plan so much in advance. I find it hard to plan for the week. I am apprehensive about that professor. Also, I won't come if your father is around."

"My father might not be around. But both my father and the professor respect musicians. Your participation would be a noble act. We usually rehearse in the chapel corridor or a house thereabout for a day or two," said Bruno

Shortly, Marta called them out for lunch. It was a hearty meal: chicken soup, rice and chicken curry, red spinach and slices of king fish fried with pepper; for desert there was *bebinca* and bananas.

Before leaving Marta asked Bruno if he would see her nieces but Caitu broke in: "Don't trouble him mama, they are not allowed to meet anyone and they are still young."

Bruno had no idea what they were talking about. Caitu reached Bruno till the end of the bund road and parted after an emotional hug.

CHAPTER XVII

Home for Christmas

1952-53 was Bruno's final year of school. He came for Christmas as planned with his aunt and her husband; Maureen was there too. Aurelia and David had by now bonded well with Bruno as if he was their own son. Three months earlier Bruno's father had left telling Ana to see that Aurelia's family had a memorable stay. They had arrived four days before Christmas. Ana sought Matilda's help. For two nights they all partook in the traditional sweet making while Matilda humored them. From 1:30 to 3:30 afternoon was siesta time.

Bruno brought Caitu over for the recitals. He had earlier spoken to the professor and the chaplain about him.

As expected families had arrived from East Africa and Bombay; their kids brought English brand of carols which suited Bruno's cousin Maureen. There was to be only two days of practice; on the second day of practice Prof. Leitão turned up. He backed Portuguese hymns with much gusto. He was both surprised and amused to see Caitu playing the banjo. The carols were a miscellany of three lingos. With no carols in the native language the chaplain and the professor refurbished a few hymns adding a Noel Noel chant to it. The English carols were the most prolific, popularized by vinyl records brought in by seafarers or Goan expatriates from East Africa. Folks also heard them on radio stations like BBC, Radio Ceylon, VOA or even radio Jakarta. Under the influence of the new anglicized kids, the native children picked them up with ease.

The third day early evening the caroling began. Though Bruno was a mediocre singer, he and Matilda ushered the troupe along the pathways, handing a lantern or lighting a candle for those that joined on the way. Starting with the few houses around the chapel the youth from these houses sang the Portuguese carols led by professor on the violin and the vocals.

As girls and boys young and old with candle-lit lanterns moved from house to house, folks came out into their balconies to welcome them. Professor who gave a head start at times faltered on the way missing a step over the uneven pathway. Caitu's strumming filled in the missed step.

Professor's house being the last the hymns he led ended there. He invited everyone into his house and treated them to snacks and gave away some money.

Before they left the Professor gave Caetano a pat and a mixed compliment:

"You play football and banjo. That is some talent. Your father is a butler. All you have to do is study well and keep away from bad company, especially your uncle Stalin. I wish you well."

He stood in the balcony until the troupe moved out of his front yard. Then an amateur violinist took over.

The small Portuguese choir, boys and girls, stayed on till the two chapel wards were done and broke off as the troupe took the bund road to go down to the Upper & Lower wards. Maureen found it a memorable trip and thanked Bruno for inviting her.

However, there was a sad end when Matilda's mother died on the last day of December.

CHAPTER XVIII

The Indian squeeze

Having done with the constitution and proclaiming the nation a democratic republic, Premier Nehru sent missives to Portugal to leave its colonies peacefully. Portugal's leader Dr. Oliveira Salazar, deeply attached to the tiny possessions earlier christened *'India Portuguesa'*, remained unyielding. In June 1953 in a retaliatory measure India closed its diplomatic mission in Delhi.

On 22 July 1954, the two tiny Portuguese-ruled exclaves of Dadrá & Nagar Haveli near Gujarat were invaded by a group of Goan revolutionaries. Portugal referred to the attackers as bandits covertly supported by India. India denied the allegation but its military refused the Portuguese to re-occupy the land-locked exclave. Enraged, the Portuguese expelled Indian consular staff from Goa and India retaliated by sealing the Portuguese consular office in Bombay. Shortly the Goa's only rail link with India was cut off and land borders sealed resulting in a total blockade of the territory. The blockade severely affected movement of people and goods between India and Portuguese territory. The regular money transfers of Goan migrant workers and the seafarers stopped. The knee jerk actions by India and Portugal put the people of the colony to severe hardship.

The Portuguese partly rescued the situation by rushing in shipments through Mormugao port. But the floodgates of covert backchannel activity were thrown open. Through land routes and waterways all kinds of players entered the fray: money-changers, smugglers, travel guides being the most prominent. A travel in an emergency became impossible leaving people at the mercy of guides, a facility that one could utilize at the risk of being robbed, swindled or in extreme cases, killed. In Goa the money-changers siphoned off 20% to convert Indian *rupiah* into Portuguese *rupia*.

After his final exam, Bruno left for Bombay planning to return home with his father. But his father extended his voyage fearing an uncertain future. Bruno's homecoming too was delayed.

CHAPTER XIX

The besieged enclave

A cloud of gloom loomed over the tiny coastal enclave. The impact on Bandar village was telling as most of its men worked in Bombay or made transit halts there during on-off shore signings. With Brazil taking over Portuguese consular services, the new registration process became stricter and lengthier. Though Indian remittances were severely restricted, Goans who worked in Africa got paid by their foreign companies; they could also land at Mormugao port avoiding the Bombay transit.

Through generations of collective farming the rural community had fostered a cooperative ethos. Though the spirit rallied them round to produce their staple diet of rice, vegetables and dairy, they were deprived of the wide variety of agricultural produce such as wheat, fine rice, lentils and fruits that weren't locally available. A few months after the blockade Matilda came over to Ana's house.

"You look worried Ana? Are you short of stuff because they stopped the border trade? Here, I brought some tinned salmon and sardines; Baltazar brought it from the Officer's mess. But tell me, any good news from your husband or Bruno?"

"Thank you Matil. Good that your brother is a guard. Well, there's good news and bad news. Bruno passed matric with a first class. He has gone to Bombay to see about his future prospects and also to meet his father. Roque has extended his contract but I haven't received his letter or the regular Money Order for three months now. What is happening Matil? Will there be a war? I just came from my mother's house this morning. A man who arrived with the help of a guide said the Indian police are asking all men in the clubs to register as foreigners; they are telling them: *'you're all Portuguese, and we have to monitor your movements. Some of you might be spying for the Portuguese."*

"A lot of rumors are floating around; yes, there could be war any time now. There are problems at both south and north border. Recently, groups of men shouting slogans tried to crash through the police cordon. The Portuguese officer was quite irritated by the Indian slogans. The police warned them not to come too close and when they did they were fired on; they fired at their legs. My brother tells me Salazar's diktat is to shoot them if they try to force in. Salazar has told the Indians they would get only burnt offerings if they try to enter by force. Oh my God! It means the end of us," moaned Matil

"But why do Indian government also suffocates us by this blockade now? What harm have our people done? No wheat, pulses, oranges or apples. In our neighborhood, there is only one Hindu family and they have two grown-up daughters. The wedding of one girl has been postponed because the saris they had ordered had not been delivered. Of course, you and I don't need them because we wear frocks, skirts and blouses ," Ana tittered

"But don't you worry Ana. My brother told me that ships have arrived at our port via Karachi with tons of goods. He tells me it is all top quality stuff: craft cheese and tinned sardines or fruit juices and fresh fruits such as apples and oranges juicier than what we get from India; and more ships are on the way with other goods like radios, cycles, cars, German or British make, all cheap," enthused Matilda

"Who told your brother about this, his *comandante?*" asked Ana as Matil blurted out:

"Oh no, the *comandante* only talks of shooting the bandits. I heard it from my other brother who lives in the port town, Vasco. He works as a foreman for the stevedores."

CHAPTER XX

Bruno Returns Home

It took a few more months for Bruno to come home. Completing his matriculation, he now carried a First Class certificate from Bombay University. Back into his mother's fold, but now an adult, he seemed a bit aloof. Ana thought it was just a loss of touch of two years.

Matilda had gone away to live with her elder brother at Vasco for a couple of months as Baltazar was put on irregular shifts and confined to his quarters. On her return, knowing Bruno had come home she rushed to Ana's house. Bruno had gone out.

"But tell me Ana, how are you doing? And why did it take so long for Bruno to return? He even missed our chapel feast. Well, as Roque has renewed his contract he could have sent you some money by now; there are other ways," said Matilda

"Yes there are ways Matil. In his recent letter he wrote to me a man would come home. And last week a man came home late in the evening wearing dark glasses and his cap pulled over his head. He gave me nine hundred rupias asking me to sign on a piece of paper. He went away but didn't tell me who he was. Soon I saw a car go by the bund road," said Ana looking blankly at Matilda

"Strange indeed! And what about your son's plans? He not only has to make his own life but has to take care of you and Roque when you are old. I hear a lot of talk about Africa. My brother tells me it's a big jungle country but gold and diamonds lie hidden that the white men are after. And our boys who go there to work for the white men make a fortune within a few years. No wonder they come back and pick up the most eligible brides around the villages. You had told me his uncle might help. Let him go. Don't keep him here for long," said Matilda

"That's the reason Bruno was delayed in Bombay. Manuel, Roque's cousin who has been working at Mombasa is to retire soon and is trying take Bruno there before he leaves. Manuel's family in Bombay has now asked Bruno to get back within a month. Looks like Manuel has worked out something better this time. His earlier two offers were not good: the first one was at a liquor shop. Roque said no way. You know he drank heavily for seven long years and gave it up after Bruno was born. It's been twenty years now and he has even helped two drunkards to give up the poison.

His second offer was worse than the first one. The job was in a gun shop. Oh my God, how terrible? There's history in my family. One of my own uncles in Bombay was sent to the Andaman," Ana broke off to sigh,

"But Bruno himself refused it for another reason. He said they kill animals with those guns. Hope he gets his call soon about the new job," she added

Matilda signaled Ana to be quiet:

"Shhhh! Don't you talk of past bad episodes? Do you mean to say Bruno has a family weakness to hit the bottle or shoot the gun? What a crazy thought? Well, forget everything and send him to Bombay to study further. If he wants to work there, let him do it. There's a bit of money there," she exhorted

Matilda lent a hand as Ana went about her chores. They had spent about an hour and it was nearing lunch time now. "And where has Bruno gone now?" she asked

"He had said he might visit that old pal of his. Did you hear anything about that boy? I know he was the prime cause for my son to be taken out of school. Bruno said it's just a casual visit to see if he is alright. Bruno tells me that boy is naïve and weak-minded. I know my son is more level headed now. And he has got a first class," said Ana beaming

"Be careful Ana. That boy's uncle is wanted by *Policia Secreta*. I heard they had almost nabbed him as he sat in Caetano's balcão. But he ran out by the backdoor under a *condo*, our coco-matted raincoat and hid among the hooded women in the field, and then escaped wearing a cassock and crossed over the border. What a clown he must be?" Matilda burst into giggly squeal as Ana simpered

"Oh I didn't hear of that. I had heard he was holding secret meetings after that Dadra incident at a village across the river Sal. But now I hear that he is injured; where and when, I don't know. Forget all that. Tell me how did you enjoy your stay at the harbor town? Must have been eating all tinned stuff. I know your brother works for the Stevedores. Things must be quiet in that corner," said Ana

"Oh yes I enjoyed my stay there playing with my brother's two kids. The harbor town seems peaceful. But I don't know if things are really quiet. My brother once talked about unknown ships keeping a watch from a distance. A Japanese sailor told him they were Indian navy ships. The Portuguese don't confront them as they have only one attack ship. The ships left after few days."

"I've heard and faced enough. Roque's father had seen two wars and Roque has seen one. They survived. Better don't talk about wars Matil. Tell me, has Baltazar come back? He must be tired and weak after months at work."

"He is at home, but will go back in three days; the same routine. He says the situation is serious in the northeast keeping police and the forest guards on their toes. There have been a few freak bombings after the Dadra attack. The miscreants sneak in near the check-posts or across the Tiracol river. But at the south end, he says, river Kali is a barrier and any movement is visible from the check-post. The Portuguese have rifles with binoculars. So they can shoot from afar."

"Stop it Matil! Tell me, now that the feast is over, what's your plan?"

"What plans to have Ana? Still, two months for the annual remembrance of my mother. I am waiting for The All Souls Day to pray for my parents," said Matilda with a sigh

CHAPTER XXI

All Souls Day

November 2nd is "All Souls Day" in the Catholic calendar. It is a day of prayer and remembrance for the faithful departed, many of whom are souls expiating their sins in a temporary abode called Purgatory, waiting to go to heaven. The bells of chapels and churches toll from morning until evening with short intervals in between. It's not the usual morning call for prayer; the typical ring is a two-tone 'ding-dong a pause ... ding-dong', though the ringing mode may vary from church to church, and also depending on the number of bells on the bell-towers.

Through the day the parishioners pour into churches, attend services, visit cemeteries, light candles and offer prayers to intercede on behalf of the poor souls of their departed. But the day is not just for the penitent souls; it is also a day to rejoice with those who are in heaven. So folks also sing joyful praises, prepare special dishes and give alms.

Two days earlier on a Sunday afternoon when Bruno returned from his cousin's, a message awaited him from the chaplain. He went to see him.

"Bruno! I am in a bit of a fix. You know the sacristan has taken ill. And my cook has suddenly left for Bombay for a job. I am a bit unwell too. I know you're a big boy now and will be leaving us soon. I wish you well. Many boys from around here are in the boarding schools. Could you find someone from your ward for half a day at least to toll the bell on All Souls Day," said the chaplain

Bruno thought for a few seconds and responded:

"I could do it myself Father, but in the afternoon. In the morning I will go to the graveyard; many of my departed have been buried there."

"You will be blessed my boy; between 3:30 to 7:15 should be fine. I will find someone for the morning session," said the chaplain

That afternoon Bruno met an elderly man who was tolling the bell. He told Bruno he is the new cook from the nearby Santa Cruz ward.

"As our villagers will be going to the cemetery in the afternoon the chaplain asked you to shut the doors by seven and hand back the keys and then you do the last toll," said the man

"I got it," replied Bruno

At seven in the evening the chapel was empty. After shutting the doors Bruno handed back the keys to the cook and rushed to the front for the last toll. He pulled the rope somewhat leisurely to let the ring resonate. As the moon beamed its first rays to greet the Bandar village Bruno felt the bell had lost its timbre. The sonorous tone he was familiar with was replaced by a flat discordant pitch.

Some 20-odd feet in the front stood a large stone pedestal with a little crucifix atop. A stooping figure emerged from there and put up a hand signaling Bruno to stop:

"Stop the bell. You've been ringing it for too long. Our night is done. We are going home," uttered a hoarse voice

Bruno stopped and let the rope go:

"You pretend to be a lost soul; I know your voice too well. What brings you here? I was expecting to go to bed early, the day being what it is, one for penitence and prayer for the dead. Did you pray for Ann Marie's soul?"

Caitu unmasked himself as he came forward:

"Ann is no more a poor soul as she is in heaven. Now, don't you know there is a drama tonight at the church ground? Speaking of penitence, the drama play is called The Penitent Pedro. It is meant for us who have been bad boys."

"You mean you more than me. You've shown it many times. But do you have the tickets?" asked Bruno

"Do we ever buy tickets Bruno? Boys throw a few stones over the fence to force the organizers to open the gates. I have done it a few times but there are bigger boys. They play it fair and wait for half an hour after the drama starts. Usually they open the gates soon after the full house. What do they lose? It's an open air theatre with lot of standing space behind. And there are lot of boys with no money and no jobs. And there are women too waiting at corners. But sometimes they take too long to open the gates and the boys get restless," Caitu snorted

Bruno took some time to decide: "Alright, we will go home first and eat something. Keep your bicycle here and we will cut across the mid bund."

Of a sudden, two men ran in towards them but sidetracked and disappeared behind the chapel.

"The guys are on the run. Do you know who they are? Someone is yelling out there. Let's go check Bruno," exclaimed Caitu

"I couldn't see their faces as they diverted. May be the guys tried to rob someone. Leave it Caitu, let's not get caught in some mix-up. I am waiting for my travel document," Bruno uttered in a cautionary tone

"I am unable to get a police clearance; so I plan to go the illegal way. But Bruno, somebody needs help out there. He is still groaning. You just lead me as you know the way and people around here," exhorted Caitu

"Since you insist on playing a detective, follow me. But Caitu, I had an eerie feeling as I did the last toll," Bruno cautioned him

They hurried across a palm grove and stopped hearing groans. The sound trail led them to a drain above which there was a banana plantation. A few plants had large stalks of bananas. The groans suddenly stopped. The clusters of leaves above made the ground dark. Bruno flashed his torch and saw foot marks in the mud. Stepping up on the slimy heap he flashed the torch on a bunch. The bananas had turned light green and two had yellowed. The bunch was half-cut at its stem and hung precariously:

"Look Caitu, the guys had almost done their job. This is Dondu's backyard. He loves his bananas more than gold," Bruno remarked to Caitu standing a few feet away by the drain

"You thieves, you have come back thinking I am dead. I am alive," a man growled from the drain

Bruno's torch beam fell on Caitu's face and then on the torso of a frail old man swaying gently holding on to the edge of the drain.

"Oh, that is Dondu," he exclaimed. As he tried to step back Bruno slipped down the slimy mud heap falling face down in the muck. He lay dazed for a moment before Caitu could lend a hand. As he picked up the torch Caitu and Dondu had got into an argument: "It's you the tall one who came with Salvador," groaned the man

"Old man, be careful, we rushed here to your help and you call me a banana-thief. I have a plantation and I could give you a bunch or two," Caitu yelled at the man

Bruno asked Caitu to step aside.

"Dondu uncle, it's me Bruno. We saw two men flee behind the chapel. But I couldn't see their faces."

"Oh it's you Bruno, Roque's son. But who is this rowdy boy? I came out hearing the bell in my kitchen and caught two loafers cutting off the largest stalk; look up there. They panicked and fled pushing me in the drain; and look they broke my chimney lamp. I know the short Salvador, a butler's son; the other one was tall like this boy. Every time I complain to the police, they ask for proof telling me it's just a banana bunch. These loafers drink and gamble and also pretend to be freedom fighters. They have robbed over a dozen bunches in the past two years." The man seemed out of breath. He resumed after a long pause:

"My son is not at home. My wife is stuck in an arm-chair and she can't hear well too, Bruno. If you will only give witness that you saw Salvador it will be enough to catch the other."

"But uncle Dondu, please don't involve me as witness. Though I've heard of Salvador I don't know him. Also, I have to leave for Bombay shortly. If you give my name the police will keep me here till your case is over. It is only a banana bunch and it is still there to pick. Now let me give you a hand to come up," Bruno pleaded

"Leave him there Bruno. A while back he was calling us thieves," snorted Caitu

"Forget it Caitu; he is a feeble old man," said Bruno and tried to pull him up but the man's feet slipped on the sandy edge. Caitu jumped in, caught the man by the haunches and hauled him up. Then he threw up his broken chimney lamp and jumped up.

Dondu sat down but seemed shaken. Under a moon beam Bruno saw the wizened face of a frail old man staring blankly at him. He tried to speak:

"Brr--- brrr ….." he stopped staring blankly at Bruno

"He is out of breath. You were quite rough on him Caitu the way you pushed him up. Now, let's put him back into his house," said Bruno

"You want be a hero by rescuing Dondu and land us at the police station. He is sure who you are, but not of the thieves. If anything happens to him they will not allow us to leave. He will be alright. Look, he is about to stand now." Caitu gave the man a hand and Bruno carried the broken lamp. But reaching his back door the man sat down on a stone border looking at his plantation.

"Dondu, is it you? What are you doing there so long? Come in now." A dry cracking voice filtered out of the door that was ajar. Dondu glanced toward the door.

Taking a cue, Bruno knocked at the door but got no response. He knocked harder and heard a rasping groan.

"Oh, Ayee Dondu is sitting here. He will come in now. I am Bruno," he cried

"What made you answer the unseen ghostly voice and tell your name?" Caitu snapped at Bruno

"Should I take you in uncle?" asked Bruno trying to hold Dondu's hand

"Brr--- brrr …" he burbled pushing away Bruno's hand and looked towards his plantation

"Dondu wants you to go away. He is quite adamant too. Let's shoot off," said Caitu pulling Bruno away by the hand

As they slunk away from the spot, Bruno grumbled:

"I hope the old man is alright. I heard he has a weak heart. They know me and my family. Dondu has high regard for my father. His son should come any time now."

"Your Dondu will manage as he has been doing. The door is not locked. And what bell was he talking about?"

"That's Dondu's alarm against banana thieves. He ties a string to the banana bunch that is about to ripen; the other end of it is tied to a bell in his kitchen. He had come out hearing the bell," Bruno explained

"Oh clever Jerry tried to outsmart the thieving Tom but he was pushed into a trench. Well Bruno, the drama starts at 8 PM. I have already eaten. Let's go, you can eat something in the bazaar."

"You want me to go in these soiled clothes? No, you come home and sit at the front while I get in through the back door and change quickly. I will take you by a different bund path by our vegetable garden."

As they detoured, dim yellow streaks of chimney lamps sneaked through the cracks of inner doors behind the windows of a few houses. They passed by a large mansion; its inner doors had not been closed. Through its glass window they could see a chandelier of oil lamps; below it a man was seated at a table cluttered with tomes. With his torso straight as an arrow and head slightly bent he was poring over a volume.

"Oh this is Prof. Leitão's mansion, I remember. What is he learning from those fat books at his age?" Caitu quipped

"He has also done law; those must be reference books,"retorted Bruno

Turning away from there, Bruno led Caitu past a few more houses. They stepped down a low but wide bund path; in the field on one side was a vegetable garden. Along the exterior of the surrounding wall was a trench filled with water. Bruno gave a rundown:

"Caitu, this is a rural ingenuity; the villagers dig up the earth and build a mud wall to protect their vegetable crop from animals. The digging leaves a trench around the wall where water collects; they use it to irrigate the crop. It is the combined effort of the village commune. We get spinach, radish, chilies, tomatoes, corn, sweet potatoes, water melons and much more."

"You are only observing Bruno. I help my mama in that work," Caitu retorted

"Bravo. My mother tells me to stay away when I offer to help," said Bruno

"Oh mama's boy," Caitu snickered

With a cascade of moon shadows over the garden land, Bruno climbed up a steep sand path and crisscrossed a few more shorter paths between houses and reached the back of the house. He signaled Caitu to go and sit at the front.

As he pushed in through the back door, he met his mother in the kitchen. She looked him up and down as he brushed past her into the bathroom.

"How did you soil your clothes?" she cried behind him

"Mãe, we came by the mid bund and cut across the low bund and then to our backside. I slipped into the water trench," he mumbled

"Who we? Who came with you?" she asked

"Caetano is with me. He's sitting in the verandah. We're going for the drama at the church. It was announced at the church and at the chapel. Didn't you hear about it?"

Ana did not respond. As he emerged all wet in his underwear she glared at him shaking her head.

"They are expecting some propaganda songs by artists from Bombay. Be careful Bruno. You have to leave in a week or two. I don't want you to get into any trouble, especially with this boy. I have heard stories about him, ask Matilda."

"Oh Matil makes her own stories mãe. I will be careful. I can handle myself. I am big now and out of school," he replied as he walked away

"What about your supper? I'll serve for both. You can call him in. I may talk but I am not cruel," she said in a firm tone

"He said he has eaten. I will serve myself, just a bite. We are in a hurry mãe."

Bruno changed into new clothes and sat to eat in haste as his mother sitting opposite him kept on cautioning him.

"Be careful, Bruno. Remember the two incidents a couple of years ago. Everybody says this boy's behavior is erratic and he is under police watch. Please don't put me under more stress," she moaned

He put his watch on and took his torch. When he was about to leave, mother pushed her hand in his shirt pocket. He didn't bother to check how much it was. He didn't want to be late for the drama.

CHAPTER XXII

THE TEATRO

The Portuguese had zealously encouraged the local converts to emulate its Latin culture in all aspects, making sure they didn't slip back into their old ways. Its end result was that the one-time homogenous community had now largely dichotomized into Catholics and Hindus. Though they looked apart the way they dressed, spoke, danced or played their music, traces of their ancestral beliefs, customs, rituals and mode of dress remained with the converts.

The two communities had now diverged into two distinct forms of drama: the Hindu *natak* and the Christian *teatro*. Each depicted its own religious identity in terms of dialect, music, dance and even stage settings. However, a song item or a character was set aside in a *natak or* a *teatro,* only to mimic the cultural and lingual idiosyncrasies of the rival to delight the largely communal audience. The village bazaar square was the regular venue for both.

But tonight's *teatro* was at the church ground. The venue and the main play 'Penitent Pedro' was perhaps appropriate on All Souls Day.

The villagers were all agog about the evening that would bring them together to watch the local artists enact a play accompanied by a string of side-shows that included a variety of solo songs, duets and some farcical hilarious rustic comedy that left them in splits. This occasional communal diversion provided the village folks an Aristotelian catharsis, a virtual release of their repressed emotions arising out of the ceaseless monotony of rustic day grind and the gloom of dark nights. But the village had its share of unemployed, school dropouts and young brats who too used the venue to indulge in their brand of fun or mischief.

Caitu biked off with his pal reaching the bazaar where a few shops were open. He thought it best to lock his bicycle and leave it there.

When the two reached the venue, not far from their school, the gates did not open as expected though the drama had progressed into Act I: a loud frenzied husband-wife quarrel could be heard over the PA horns. The venue between the Christ monument and the cemetery was covered all around by a high bamboo-matting with a canopy of cloth sheets overhead; two manned gates, one near the front and another at the back were the entry points for the ticket-holders.

Outside the venue youth strolled up and down or hung about at vantage points, from church front to the monument, to the cemetery wall. Others sat under the two gulmohar trees. In the school verandah a group of women lay huddled. All waited in hope that gates would be thrown open.

This was the mid 1950s when the little colony had no electricity except in the heart of its few district towns. So for most people on an occasion like this, it was left to the

German invention, the Petromax, to light up their dark nights. The kerosene operated Petromax not only found a long lease of life in most Portuguese-held colonies but had a virtual 'let there be light' outreach to most parts of the underdeveloped and rural world.

Bruno tried to keep pace as Caitu hurried round the fenced wall keeping a roving eye at corners. Moving closer to the gate he tried to peep in annoying the gateman who was dealing with a group of ticket holders.

"Boy, what are you looking in for? Do you have a ticket?" asked the gateman

"I am trying to see if my girlfriend is already in. I have to pass an urgent message from her family," said Caitu in a serious tone

"Oh! Is it? Give us her name. We will make an announcement," the man snapped back

"Let me check first, she might be still out," said Caitu and walked off

"He made a fool of you Caitu," Bruno taunted

"Let's look around; I think they won't open the gates soon."

Moving away, they stopped by the gulmohar tree seeing Ronnie and Bonnie, the inseparable duo, seated with a group of boys.

"You are late Caitu. They are almost at the end of Act I and haven't opened the gates yet," said Ronnie juggling a pebble

"Wasn't there any wedding tonight? You juggle well. Flinging stones with precision is tougher. And do you have to wait for me always?"

"Nothing of the sort; I am only a dancer. One can't be good at everything like you. And mind you they have put up a cover above. You will have to do it from close range but you shouldn't hurt anyone. They are our own families," said Ronnie

"Don't give a sermon on do's and don'ts, Ronnie. If you can't do it keep quiet about it."

As a unruly gang of boys suddenly queued up at the hind gate. One of them took the gateman aside and spoke into his ear and then pushed his folded palm into his hand. The man pocketed it and pushed the boys in. Caitu turned round hearing someone call out his name.

"Hello Pascal, the gatekeeper is pocketing a few *rupias* there. I think the tickets have been sold out. They should be opening the gates any time now," said Caitu as Ronnie butted in:

"Greedy guys, they might make us wait till half way. Check these pebbles I had gathered Caitu; have a few more in my pocket."

Caitu picked and threw down the stones, pocketing a few smaller pebbles. He cautioned Ronnie: "Do you want me to knock people's head off and turn it into a disaster?"

Pascal sounded an alert:

"Caitu it's high time we act. Act 1 is about to end any moment. I will be on the side of graveyard wall and you stick around here. We will do our act as Act 1 ends and the band starts to play. Be swift in throwing: five little pebbles in ten seconds; wait for five seconds, fling another three and then scoot off to the bazaar. I will follow you there. We've done this before, didn't we?" Pascal walked away after Caitu gave a punch of approval.

Caitu pulled Bruno aside: "You wait here. If they open the gates go in with them. Do not wait for me." He winked at him and walked off.

In few a minutes Act I came to an end; then a burst of drum roll as the brass quartet pumped out a medium swing trot. There was some shouting inside. Pushing the gates open men charged out with torch-lights yelling. One of them came up to Bonnie:

"Who's throwing stones inside. Did you see anyone? The inspector is sitting inside. We'll get the police to act," he blurted out

"I didn't see anyone; what an evil act indeed? Anyway, we are enjoying the music and the songs; it sounds good enough from here. The guy who did it could have run to the river side or inside the church compound."

The red herring Bonnie had thrown made the man swear and rush to the church front; another ran to the monument.

Soon an announcement blared on the horn speakers:

"Oh people, on a solemn occasion like today, All Souls Day, we appeal to you to stop this unholy act. Please stop throwing stones. There are families with elderly and children sitting inside. People have been injured."

There was an eerie silence and after a few minutes the loudspeaker blared again:

"Attention people! We are pleased to announce that the gates are now open. Those who wish to come in may do so by the back gate only and stand well clear of the seated guests."

The announcement sparked a mad rush of people: men, boys and kids pushed through the gate watched by two gatekeepers. The last to walk in was a group of women and shy giggly girls; a few had their faces covered under shawls.

Inside, the simulated drama hall, from the stage to the last row of seats, was lit up by Petromax lamps hung on poles. Also tied to the poles were funnel shaped PA horns, their blaring sounds tearing into the still of the night.

Act I of the main play having just ended a huge maroon drop-curtain had come down.

The band, a brass quartet backed by a banjo player and a drummer had taken a spot below the stage; behind them in the first row were the dignitaries that, as a custom, included the priests, the regidor, the prominent elders and the police. Behind them were a crowd of the three main villages, and quite a few were from across the river. Right behind were the lately arrived ticketless standees.

A *teatro* with high melodrama and a variety side show would be the talk of village for days to come.

Once inside, as Bonnie and his gang scrambled behind a huddle of younger females, Bruno excused himself and moved to the wider open area on one side where a bunch of kids had squatted; he could well pretend to be one of them.

It was time for the band to play. The drummer cracked a short roll and got into a quick trotting tempo with the banjo strumming along. As the saxophonist and the clarinetist did the intro, the trumpeters joined in to pump out raucous tune. In seconds, two clowns in gaudy attire with painted faces emerged from either side of the curtain, hopping and skipping animatedly. One was a male in Charlie Chaplin garb, wearing a coat, a hat with a stick in hand; his partner with lipstick and rouged cheeks wore a knee-length can-can skirt and a tight blouse with pointed bras, his legs covered with pink stockings. The kids seemed to enjoy every moment of it, trying to subdue their cackles for fear of being rebuked. But a few adults laughed even louder.

The end of the raucous hilarious act brought its desired response: a furious burst of handclapping, cat-calling and shouts of encores. They came back and dida verse and a chorus, entirely new and got the same response with encores but they didn't come again.

Realizing that Caitu hadn't come in yet Bruno first checked with Bonnie's gang and then went out and looked around. Getting no clue he returned to the kids; they were quiet now as the Act 2 played out a rather morose scene with Pedro on a hospital bed alone ranting in lament.

*"I see the walls collapsing around me; another moment I am battling the ocean all alone; there isn't a way out... not only wife left me but also my children....no friends come and see me....only a few drunkards who laughed and made merry with me.....but all they say.........***enters a priest and sits beside Pedro*****.....** *"Father you know I worked hard, I didn't cheat or steal nor hurt anyone.....but, may be, drank a peg more for joy and sadness...otherwise I've been faultless"........***Stop Pedro,*** *"Faultless you said!.... Let me begin...here count the faults as I lay them bare to you"....*

The scene unnerved Bruno as he thought about Caitu. *'Why is he taking so long? He and Pascal must have surely gone to some pub to do the shots'* he thought. He let the thought fleet off. Two boys right next to him began chatting quietly.

"Aren't you interested in the play," Bruno asked

"Oh it is quite boring don't you think? It's for the old folks. We prefer the songs and the comedy," one of them quipped

Time passed by and the drama advanced ending Act II but there was no sign of Caitu. Bruno got worried well knowing Caitu was a teatro-phile. He couldn't understand the reason behind his delay. *'Oh the two must be still doing the shots at the pub. I wish he was here to listen to Pedro.'* The thought nagged him.

With a break from the main play, a well-known singer did a moralizing solo followed by a duet by a male-female duo-- a real one this time. '*The man was about to sail away after getting married. While she moaned she would be alone again, he wondered whether she would remain devoted to him.*' It was a question-answer duet.

As Bruno kept his focus on the stage, a random image of Dondu standing in the ditch flashed in his head triggering a thought flow: '*I hope he is alright. How could we leave him out there and walk away? It was my fault. And now this Caitu hasn't returned. Maybe they nabbed him whilst throwing stones.*'

A glance towards the gate put a stop to his speculation. He rushed to meet him. Caitu's face seemed uncharacteristic as he avoided looking him in the eye.

Whining, Bruno quizzed him: "Where had you been? Did they catch you throwing stones? Or someone mugged you?"

Caitu snorted, and pulled Bruno aside by the elbow signaling that they should go out:

"Me, mugged? I haven't met my match yet," he cried with bravado, and added:

"Let's go and sit by the gulmohar tree. I have something to tell you. Nothing serious, though." He let out a girlish snigger this time, an uneasy kind. As they came out, they noticed a policeman standing under the gulmohar and Caitu suggested they get across the road and move to the riverside. Bruno felt that was even more uncharacteristic.

"What's wrong with you? You have missed two Acts of the play and lots more of the sideshow and now you want to miss what's left. You brought me for the drama, didn't you?" Bruno's tone was plaintive.

"Come come! Things do happen. I will tell you in a moment," mumbled Caitu in a nervy tone

They stepped on the road between the church front and its bifurcated cemetery. Through the open gate in the sheltered section they could see a few candles burning still.

CHAPTER XXIII

Musing by the bank of Adnem, the side river

In a minute they made it to the river bank, the very spot they had come two years ago; to the left was the administrative building adjoining the priests' residences and *Comunidade* offices. A few meters down to the right a little silver painted canoe swayed gently. Further away was the ferry. As they sat down they noticed the striking changes: the road had moved away and piers and supports jutted out of the waters across the width of the river; nearby from a large storehouse they heard voices amid clangs of striking metal.

"Bruno, you know what they're up to," said Caitu

"They are building a bridge. Leitão says in a year's time we will have a beautiful bridge to last a hundred years. No more canoeing across or long winding road for all the villages right up to Cape of Rama. Taxis, cars, trucks and busses from your side will go by this bridge to the district town. Leitão also said bigger bridges are coming soon."

"Too little too late Bruno. Almost everybody knows the end is near. It's no more a secret that India is sure to push Portuguese out?" retorted Caitu

"But how and when? Prof. Leitão says it will only happen over our dead bodies. Salazar is adamant and will not give up," Bruno grumbled

The waters of the swelling tide reflected a shimmering bright golden moon that was rising up in the south-east sky and the silver canoe to their right began to swing in jerks.

"Who left that nice canoe there I wonder? We could have a ride," Caitu mused

"Tell me Caitu, what did we come here for? You said you wanted to tell me something. What is it? We are missing the drama." Bruno seemed irritable

Caitu fell silent as he gazed at the waters. Of a sudden he got up and strode near the canoe and untied the rope from the peg it was tied to. Pulling the canoe closer, he sat down and pushed his long leg down into the boat and stepped into the boat. He picked up the paddle and rowed the boat near Bruno.

"Come Bruno, let's go for a little ride. I always wanted to view your church precincts from the river. Boys who came to our school by ferry used to tell us it looked like fortress. Hop in now," he exhorted

Bruno tried to talk him out of his rash move: "How can you use someone's canoe without their permission? We could be in trouble. You might capsize the boat. Will you never learn Caitu?"

"You're safe Bruno. You know I can paddle a boat as good as I pedal my cycle. We would be back after a few minutes. Come on Bruno," Caitu pleaded

After some hesitation Bruno got in.

"Alright, now let me give you a cruising view of your church from the back side." As he tried to turn the boat, his hurried back pushes veered the canoe back towards pillars.

"Be careful Caitu, you are going backwards. Don't get into another misadventure by hitting the pillar; the water is still filling upstream," Bruno cried

"Don't worry. I've handled bigger country boats. The problem is this one is too light Bruno."

He managed to turn the boat round and moved forward staying close to the bank. Passing by the tall wide gray plastered wall along the river's narrow grassy bank, he pointed to the two small windows high up.

"What lies behind this huge wall? It looks like an ancient monastery I told you," he exclaimed

"On top in one block lies the church office; we get all our certificates, from birth to baptism, and marriage or death. Further inside is the priests' residence. But to get there you have to climb up a long wide staircase. On the other side, there are the Comunidade offices.

Down below on the ground floor is the real dungeon with many rooms mostly empty. I had been there a few times," said Bruno

"So you only should know everything Bruno. Let me also see a few things I haven't seen. This place has a history you know?" he said in a taunting tone

"I've seen a few rooms down and a few things. I don't know everything. But you're taunting for what. It is our church. Past is long gone," Bruno snapped back

Going past the large walled structure they went by a garden porch, where by the water's edge stood a tiled roof shed. Eyeing a landing slide further ahead, Caitu paddled with more vigor. Reaching it, he thrust the boat up asking Bruno to step out. As Caitu was the boatman Bruno remained at his mercy. They got out and Caitu tied the boat to a wooden peg.

"Oh Bruno, my boat did a smooth landing. We've reached the little garden," Caitu crowed

"Firstly, this is not your boat. You know, for centuries until a few decades ago the priests used to come by boat and land here. There were no motor cars, only bullock carts for the common man and palanquins for the few nobles," Bruno responded

"Oh, the nobles; who were they? Good that you know a lot of Portuguese history. Let's go in there and explore now," said Caitu

It was a small porch by the bank with a scatter of decorative plants and a few more potted ones; overlooking it was the open gateway of a long sacristy corridor. Caitu walked to the lone shed by the water and tried to push the door open. It was locked from inside. Bruno cautioned him.

"Don't push the door. There might be someone inside." Bruno kept his voice low.

"Someone inside? It is pitch dark in there," said Caitu retracing his steps

"I'd been there once to pee. The hole slides into river."

"And what's there at the extreme end beyond the landing?" asked Caitu

"There are couple of store rooms for dozens of marble statues, some of them life size."

"And that half-open narrow door of the monastery? "

"Caitu, don't give your own names; inside are many rooms mostly empty; boys used to call it a dungeon. I told you what is above it."

Asking Bruno to hold on Caitu walked into the long corridor and paced up and down seemingly inquisitive. When he came back he found Bruno missing and the dungeon door shut. Caitu pushed it open and entered a dark empty room. Seeing a streak of dim light, he walked into the next room. He found Bruno standing by a table with a small chimney lamp. He was frisking through pamphlets.

"What are you going through those catechism books for? Your time is past it. Catch the lamp and let's explore" said Caitu

"What's wrong with you? Let's go back for the drama," Bruno grumbled but Caitu pushed him on:

"Let's make a quick run through the rooms; we might find something to eat. I am hungry," he said picking up the lamp

As they moved from one empty room to another it seemed like an endless and pointless search; most rooms had no doors. "These are like many little Pandava caves Bruno," uttered Caitu

"I had not come this way and this far before. Please go back to where we started from."

"I don't know which way I had come," Caitu grumbled

Bruno took the lamp from him and turned back right and then left.

"Since the lamp was lit, the priest should be around. We could ask for water and something to munch," said Caitu

"Don't be stupid; you have encroached here; it's an offence and immoral too," Bruno retorted

They came into a larger room and found a decrepit broken boat that had half its mast and one torn sail. Bruno brought the lamp closer.

"Do you remember the caravela with the triangular sails we saw in the movie two years ago? That's the one. I don't know who had come in this, perhaps the first priest or someone significant," Bruno mused, grinning under the lamp light

Turning round into another room they saw lying on a table a partly open box marked Caritas Internationalis. There were sealed pouches of brown paper; Caitu eyed two that were open, one of biscuits and another with milk powder.

"I am really hungry; biscuits and even milk powder will do," said Caitu pushing biscuits in his pocket. He scooped some powder with his palm and lapped it.

"Have some biscuits at least Bruno," he muttered, choking with milk powder. They heard a hoarse muffled cough emanating from the garden porch.

"Stop it Caitu? Won't you ever learn? Let's go away from here. There's someone out there in the garden. On the right the dungeon leads to another door exiting into a little garden that opens to the front yard of the church."

"That's great. Put the lamp down and let's walk out from the front then," Caitu urged

"No way Caitu! We cannot leave the boat there. Let's face the music if we have to. Come follow me."

With a bit of Bruno's guidance, they walked through a number of open doors and finally found the room where Bruno first was. Bruno put back the lamp and they exited the main door.

Not finding anyone in the garden, they hurried across and got into the boat. Caitu tried to paddle away swiftly but got close to the lone shed and ended up brushing the boat against the sliding hole that lay a little above the water level.

"Look, there is the pig toilet here. There's an awful smell coming out from it."

"Dumb boy, pigs don't go swimming in the river. It is the river latrine. I heard it has been there for centuries even though it could have been renovated many times. Didn't I tell you I had peed in there once? I had to rush in there when my mother had brought me for confirmation ceremony," exclaimed Bruno

"Thank God, you didn't slip through into the river," Caitu giggled

Instantly, they heard the coughing, followed by a loud sound of someone passing the wind. Caitu quickly steered the boat away and headed back laughing all the way. They disembarked, tied up the boat and then stood a bit stunned at what they just did.

As they stood on the bank they heard echoes of a dialogue rippling across the water.

"It was a purposeless escapade Caitu. Let's go back now."

"Wait a second. I had brought you here to tell something. And I'm still not through with it. It will take a few minutes. Sit for a couple of minutes only." Caitu's tone was a murmur this time.

As they sat down Bruno tittered as he recalled:

"Caitu! I wonder who could be using the latrine in the night. The priests have their washrooms upstairs where they live. It is mostly used by parishioners during the church services."

"Ghosts are still out as the night isn't done yet. Forget the damn latrine and that son of a devil in there," cried Caitu, and now, let me tell you what I had to tell. It is about Dondu," he mumbled again

Just then they heard that cough again, so close behind them it made them turn; an indistinct figure loomed in and stood a few feet away behind them. He was a bare-chested sinewy man with sun-burnt skin; under the moonlight his dark eyes glared at them. He was in shorts. He shuffled his feet to feel the grass and then spoke in a hoarse but clear voice:

"Boys! I don't know why you came there after grabbing that boat."

"We did it just for fun. Are you the owner of the boat?" asked Caitu

"I can well say I am. So you not only stole a boat but also encroached on the church property in the night like thieves, committing two offences. Not to say it wasn't risky as you could have toppled over and drowned. But I won't file any complaints against you. I too have children," he said in a softer tone

"We know to swim. But, who are you?" asked Caitu

The man then announced his identity merrily:

"I am Pedru, the grave digger. I also blow the coronet during feast days. I am very tired because I had to dig two graves yesterday, and then to fill them up again. But I am happy because I earned a bit more. Mind you, no ill-feelings for the living or the dead. Not many are dying these days and that makes my life harder."

The boys could sense the man was tipsy but stable on his feet. He shuffled his feet again and squatted on the grass. Caitu stood up, a bit agitated:

"Man, you had a few shots, I know. But be careful how you talk. You want people to die so that you live? Are you a vulture?" As Bruno tried to calm Caitu down, Pedru stood up:

"Oi! Are you threatening me? I am not scared of the dead or the living. It's not your business to tell me how I should speak. Take your seat," he hollered as Caitu sat down looking sheepish

Pedru sat down and resumed in a firm but calmer tone:

"I am authorized to keep a watch around the church precincts. With whose permission you took that private boat? And what are you doing at this time of the night? The village Regidor and the Vicar have asked me to do the night vigil around here, especially because there's a lot of stuff lying around for the bridge they are building here."

"And did I hear you say some son of a devil was in that damn latrine. I am that son of the devil who buries your bodies to rot in the ground. And that god-damn latrine you said. But don't you know there's history to that latrine?"

Bruno engaged the man with his habitual calm:

"We didn't mean to be rude to you, brother. We know it's your job and a hard one too. I saw the graveyard. It's so calm and peaceful with the graves so neatly kept. But still, it wasn't nice when you said not many people were dying these days."

The man was swift to respond:

"I like your tone of speech. Yes the yard is calm and peaceful because beneath lie only the dead bodies. The earth dissolves everything that comes under its comforting arms. It treats man and animal with no grudge or favor." As he stretched his legs he pulled out a pint from his pocket.

"I've had a quarter already. I will have a bit more and go eat some food," he added

"You speak like a philosopher Pedru. You had a quarter and then walked twenty-six steps up and twenty-nine down the twin stairways; you could have stumbled," said Bruno with concern

"Oh clever boy, you have counted the steps. I didn't come by the stairway. I came out through the dungeon. I had the keys because the sacristan is sick. But I go up and down those steps every day though I wonder why they did that. They have to make sure the priests who come here are young and fit. When I asked the priest he told me the road to heaven is a tough road. You may think it's only with us Christians. Once I visited a Hindu temple on the Paroda hill. I had to climb five hundred steps to reach the temple. I was told each step washes a sin. But most churches the Portuguese built are on ground level so that even the lame could enter. That was good."

"Why did you go to a Hindu temple? Did you feel cleansed after that?" asked Bruno feeling provoked and amused by gravedigger's talk

"I accompanied a Hindu who claims to be my cousin brother. He says we have descended from the same ancestors. He lives on the border of Bandar village." They were distracted by a surge of sounds on the water.

"Good harmonic duet! The drama is happening behind us but the sounds seem to come from across the banks. When the water is calm it will sing with us; when it is rough it will choke our voices. I wanted to watch the play as it is about Pedro, my namesake, who is condemned to repent. Anyway, boys, when I said not many deaths these days, I only stated a fact. I don't wish anyone to die and they don't die because of me. This tough job of digging and filling up the graves is a kind of repentance for me. I give the dead some dignity, seeing that their graves remain neat and that no weeds or wild grass grow atop as the folks rest below. I have a family to feed too," Pedru paused to cough

"He's right Caitu. He's had a tough day digging two graves. Though he looks strong he is not a young man any more. He seems quite a guy and worth listening too." said Bruno giving Caitu a nudge. Then he turned to Pedru:

"I know this church has history as it is about 350 years old. We also heard the Portuguese built a fortress here before the church. Now that should have some history. I have read a bit and heard a bit from the priests and my

professor. But what history could a latrine make?" asked
Bruno

CHAPTER XXIV

The Untold Story from the mouth of Witness

Pedru glanced at the moon and then across at the silvery sheen of the water. Picking up the pint beside him he uncapped it and took a swallow, recapped it and put it down. Bruno sensed that Caitu was getting restless or bored. Pedru resumed:

"But I heard things in bits and pieces; the priest told me the Portuguese set foot here four hundred years ago in *caravela* boats with two sails. There is one such broken boat lying in one of the rooms below the priests' residence. I often wonder how they faced the mighty seas and the strong winds with that fragile boat. The winds of this little river have blown off the roof of my house twice. I can't read the fat history books but I can read quicker the 'sol fas' to play coronet and the drums.

Now you could have heard or read from books of what exactly happened here." He sipped again from the pint as Bruno responded:

"Pedru, we call this stream 'Adnem' – or '*ad nuim*', a side river; on this side of Sal lie our three villages. Twenty years after landing on the banks of Mandovi the Portuguese reached here. Noting the rich human and agricultural resources of our villages, they built an outpost or a little fort to oversee its rule and trade.

But I have read of the confrontation fifty years later at Kunkali that ended with the killing of five priests and a few others; they were slain by swords by Hindu chiefs who later requested to reconcile. Ignoring their pleas for a few months, Portuguese later invited the chiefs for negotiations at the fort. They were called in two batches over a period of two months. But some tragedy happened. I cannot say anything more because nothing is written as to what and how it happened." Bruno kept quiet.

"Well my friends, you very well know the root cause of that confrontation; Portuguese started a conversion drive, destroyed the temples and erected crosses or churches in its place."

Caitu whispered in Bruno's ear:

"That's an old story we all know. Let's get away from here. The man is talking over sips. We have our own problems. You will not like what I have to tell you. We can have a drink on the way. The bars may close."

Pedru cut in: "what is it boys? You talk about bars. But this is an untold story that is not written in your books," he said in a serious tone as Caitu butted in:

"Pedru! Tell us your untold story but make it short. Yes, I do drink sometimes but my friend doesn't. I might have a shot at Jackinas bar."

"Jackinas bar may close by then. There's quite a bit left in the pint, you may have it. But I hope you won't be offended by my offer. I am a grave digger, man of another tribe. I don't know what your tribe is," said Pedru pitching up his voice as Caitu responded:

"My villagers tell me we belong to the warrior tribe though we are Christians. But I am also a socialist in thought and deed. So I treat you both as a comrade and brother. Why do you think low of being a grave-digger or inferior to a warrior tribe?" Caitu got up and paced gingerly to Pedru who held out the pint to him. He took two deep sips and returned to the seat.

Pedru chuckled and interrupted with a mocking tone:

"Ah Ah! The warrior tribe! Those who killed the priests were of the same tribe. Many of them became converts and got rewarded. You are their descendents." He grinned showing two missing teeth. He resumed spiritedly:

"So, you didn't fight the Portuguese like warriors. You only subjugated smaller weaker clans. The Hindu relative told me an amusing story of your tribe. He *said long before the Portuguese your ancestors marched into this land like the ants and took over garden lands and the nearby tillable land and pushed our older tribes into the wetlands or the hills. The Rajas were of your tribe. So they sided with you.*

Your ancestors danced with the umbrellas parading their deities on the ladders. They kept us away but watched us from a distance and copied our ways: like the feast on the full moon day, and the worship of the white-ant hills. They were amazed by our all-powerful deity, Betal, the lord of the demons but treated him as their god's sidekick. But there was also a tribe above you, who claimed that the gods only spoke to them. They were the advisers of your Rajas.

Then the Portuguese came in pretending to be the savior of all tribes to release them from the clutches of the Moors. You opened your arms to them but soon they began destroying your temples and deities; you tried to fight but you were overcome; those who couldn't fight fled in the interior or beyond the borders with their deities. You who were left behind were lured and subdued. They converted you and taught you to eat meat and drink wine and taught you a different dance, not holding the umbrellas but holding your womenfolk. You remained content and forgot to fight." Pedru ended with a chuckle as the boys intervened:

Caitu put up his hand: "Wait, did your Hindu great-grand cousin told you all this?"

"Pedru, you shouldn't be the talebearer of your Hindu cousin as you are a Christian like us," added Bruno

"Yes indeed. My cousin mocked me saying I too am a convert who eats meat, drinks wine and dances with my women." Pedru guffawed and then continued.

"Now since you're in a hurry I will begin my untold story. My version is not found in any books. The notings that few Jesuits had made were burnt or taken away by them when they were packed off from the colony. But there were participants and witnesses who lived on. And what they did or saw caused them distress. So they spoke in their sleep, whispered to the wind, told a close friend or their children. Their children then told their children and on, and on." Pedru coughed and put his hand where his pint was earlier. He chuckled as his hand caught a tuft of grass. Caitu had put the pint on the right side.

"Sorry Pedru, I didn't know you're left-handed. But it's real hard stuff. It burned my throat. Please begin the real story," said Caitu cheerfully

Pedru gulped the remnant and flung the pint into the river. He spat and glanced at the moon and then at the water.

"Yes, it was around this time of the year. It could be on this day itself. The same moon up shining on the waters would now be a witness as I speak; we humans think it is speechless but the river and the moon talk to each other all the time, day and night. Whenever I sit here alone I hear murmuring voices: commands and accusations and begging pleas." Pedru got up and walked to a coconut tree to urinate.

Caitu whispered to Bruno: "commands and accusations? I hope he is not hearing voices in his head. Next, he may hear a command to push us down the bank." Bruno told him to shut up. Pedru came back and resumed as he sat down:

"What I am telling you is exactly what happened that day inside the walls of the fortress and not the walls of the church which didn't exist then. The fortress was extended soon after the confrontation."

"Go on Pedru. The drama must be past half-way. So we have some time," said Caitu

Pedru belched before he spoke:

It was a small but longish fortress extending from east to west divided in the middle into south front and the river-

side north. The front section had a gate with a watch tower; inside it on the east, there was a waiting room, the Comandante's office and an amusement room. Facing the rooms was a longish yard for daily drills; at its end lay a little chapel and beyond it was a burial yard at the west end. This was the front section of the fort.

The riverside inner section was separated by a wall with a gate in the middle. Facing the inner gate was a garden and two small latrines by the water's edge; towards the west end was the boat landing and then the burial yard. On the east side, that is where we are now, there was a two-storeyed structure, a mess-room and two rooms for the officers.

A month after the killing of five priests and the laymen, the ten village Hindu chiefs got a second invitation offering a peace deal. This was a month after six of their colleagues who came earlier for talks had been detained.

That afternoon the ten chiefs of Kunkali came in a caravan of bullock carts with their followers. At the gate they were met by very warm and friendly guards. As the small crowd waited out a native appeared at the gate with a message:

"The Comandante welcomes you on a day of great expectation, a day to forget enmity and live in peace as brothers. But as there are differences between your leaders themselves, the talks may take time. So except for the ten leaders all others should disperse and go home."

The native then read out names of five men, the main suspects in the killing of the priests. He told them to leave their swords behind before entering.

The followers became agitated asking their leaders not to go in without their swords. They also demanded to see the six of their men detained earlier. One of the chiefs then conveyed the same to the native who exchanged a word with the guards at the gate.

The native then told the chief that he would convey the demand to the Comandante and will return soon. He didn't turn up for a long time as two armed guards stood by the gate.

Meanwhile, the ten chiefs retreated to their carts to have refreshments that the followers had brought. It was approaching evening as the chiefs and their followers sat there waiting.

The guards kept yelling at the crowd to go away: "Vai, vai embora, vai todos para casa." A few of them left.

Then a guard yelled asking the chiefs to come forward as the native showed up at the gate. He spoke as they came up:

"The Comandante has accepted your demands; you may keep your swords with you f a s t e n e d to the waist and come in one by one. Once you're in you will be joined by your six colleagues in the waiting room."

Caitu stood up to interrupt but Bruno pulled him down as Pedru resumed:

The ten men were allowed in. Once inside things seemed even calmer; no soldiers paraded in the yard; towards the far end a few bearded men wearing robes stood in front of the chapel conversing.

"So many priests today?" remarked Kalia in a tone of concern as they were directed to the waiting room.

"Because it's a peace meeting" said Mulgo

The guard had no idea what the Hindu men were talking about. He led them into a narrow boxy room with two little grilled windows high above the wall and made them to sit on two benches. As he left two African men stood outside the door. It was a long agonizing wait as they couldn't see what was happening in the yard. Gradually whispers of men and occasional sharp tones filtered in. Then another native, a nervous wiry man appeared at the door:

"Brothers! The Comandante is now ready to meet you; he waits for you along with your six colleagues in the mess hall behind the inner gate; he wishes that the five most respected of your leaders appear first. Do come forward as your names are called out. You may keep your sword but let it stay fastened to the waist. The Comandante sends you his best wishes on this auspicious day."

The man walked away and a soldier in uniform appeared calling out the five chiefs.

As the ferocious five were escorted out, the other five kept waiting. Minutes followed with only dead silence as the five who waited became restless and agitated. They heard whispers of unknown tongue behind the door followed by a random yell or a grouch from afar. Then over the high grill window a familiar but distant voice filtered in:

"Kalia, Gopi, Vasu, all five of you ...come out and get away!" .... a hoarse grouch followed

Vasu was the first to jump up in panic, alerting the four in the room:

"Something isn't right Gopi. That sounded like Ramgadd. He's telling us to escape. Pull out your swords and barge out"

As the first two tried to push the door it appeared to be barred from the outside. The five of them then crashed at it a few times and it broke open. The five burst out slashing their swords in the air but three African soldiers wielding an axe and curved knives diverted the two into a side lane.

Kalia, Gopi and Bicu ran towards the main gate but found it closed with three young soldiers standing with carrack swords in hand. They stood firm with stern faces but didn't make a move to attack. The three then turned back towards the inner gate but now another spectacle caught their sight; the colleague who had alerted them was now fighting two robed men.

"Look that's Ramgadd for sure....the robed priests are attacking him but he has slain one of them. He needs our help." As they rushed to his aid he shouted back:

"Bavu!.... go away, escape to fight another day...... they have slain three of our braves. Curse on them. But I and the brave Wagha will take on as many of these barbarians before we go...."

"Oh yes! There I see Wagha still battling two of them in the burial yard. The two robed men are gloating over our three braves lying on the ground," cried Gopi

They went closer to Ramgadd whose upper garment was torn and soaked with blood. They were confronted by three men who emerged from behind the chapel. Leaping aside, Ramgadd yelled at his colleagues:

"Bavu, go away from here. We have been betrayed. Let the curses of the Five Deities and Betal be on our traitors. Wagha and I have slain three of them. I will take one or two more. I've been destined to die for my faith. But I want you to stay alive to protect it. Climb the walls or jump in the river."

The three retreated from the chapel to the centre.

"Gopi, Bicu, look to our right in the lane, our two brothers have been felled in the lane," cried Kalia

Unable to look at their fallen comrades, the three were caught between fierce rage and deep emotion.

There was only the inner gate to turn to. By now the sky was overcast and it started to rain. They pushed the door of the inner gate and it creaked open. On the east side a lane passed between the two-storey structure and small rooms; on the west side by the boat landing two African men stood with bow-and-arrow and machete slung to their waists. Right in front there was a kind of wild garden with flower plants overgrown with bush clumps; at the river's edge stood two small latrines.

Only the bursts of wind and rains gave the three men some respite. They hung on not knowing which side to turn

"There's a storm gathering now. Let's lie down and crawl between the bushes, they are not making a move to corner us yet," whispered Kalia to his colleagues

There was a sudden bluster of wind gusts emitting swooshes, knocks and bangs. Gopi and Bicu crawled down toward the right and rushed through the lane to get to the bank; they were suddenly pulled away by men from behind.

The slim and dark skinned Kalia crawled inching forward even as he heard the cries of his two colleagues. A soldier walked past him almost stamping on his hand. As he went away Kalia crawled into a bush. He could see a latrine by the water's edge few feet away. A soldier rushed out buttoning his shorts.

Of a sudden a huge wind blast lifted the roof of one of the latrines sending it crashing towards the group of soldiers behind making them run for cover. In a flash, Kalia surged forward and slipped into the latrine and locked the door. Its roof was intact.

Peeping through a hole he noticed the two African men had also walked away to escape the flying debris. A little away two men in a caravela struggled to keep stable as winds kept rolling the boat and throwing them off balance. Kalia heard the cries of agony of his two companions as they exhaled the last breath one by one. Then he heard a knock on the door and a shout: 'Quem está dentro ái ...sai..sai apresse.' He knew a soldier wanted to relieve himself. The shouts turned louder with him not responding. Then the knocking became furious. Kalia knew there was no time left for him.

He bent down on his knees by the commode and peered into the shithole. The fetid toxic fumes assailed his nostrils. Gazing deeper he was awestruck. It was a rectangular 1 ft by 2 ft hole with a 4 ft. stone slide. The bottom of the slide lay under water. With a strong will to survive, he was struck by a flash idea. It was no shitty idea, though.

He squeezed himself through the hole and slipped down the slide into the water. The wind and the patter of the rain drowned the splash and he was in the river. Though he had slipped in unnoticed, Kalia couldn't risk swimming in the open downstream where boat lay in wait. The men would certainly come after him or the Africans could shoot him with a poison arrow. Then he saw two boats on east side upstream. His only option was to go underwater way ahead of the boat landing and beyond the burial yard. Kalia had swum underwater many times in the Galgibaga and had once swum the wide mouth of the mighty Kali before he became a village chief. But he knew it would be tough under the murky water. He wouldn't know where he was heading to. He wasn't also sure what lay beyond the burial yard. He had heard many of the villagers were new converts.

A late evening overcast sunless sky gave him another flash idea. He swam the width of the river underwater in a diagonal line and ending up under a mangrove on the opposite bank. Grief-stricken, he hung on mourning his fallen friends in the comfort of the vast swamp of wilderness. As night descended, with a run here and swim there, he finally reached the Kunkali village. Of the ten and six he was the only one that got away.

"There the story ends my friends," said Pedru aloud

Caitu was feeling uneasy as though he wanted to move. Pedru lifted himself up with some difficulty.

"Oh my bones, they are a bit stiff. Doctor says it is the acid from drinking *feni*. I think I should go now. There is not a sound. The drama has ended perhaps," said Pedru

"Tell me Pedru? What they did with the bodies? I heard they were ferried in a caravela to Anjediva island," said Caitu

"Such stories are still going around. Taking bodies many miles away through a turbulent coast was a risk and waste of time. Moreover, Anjediva is a graveyard island that swallows people alive. My ancestor had lived there.

But things had to be done in haste. With a workforce of soldiers and hired men it wasn't a great task. The truth I know of is that nine bodies of the Hindu chiefs are buried beneath the dungeon," uttered Pedru with a tone of finality

"And while all this happened weren't there people outside the fort? And how the robed priests could kill the unarmed men?" Bruno interjected

"You're the thinking boy. The followers left as the weather got bad leaving behind three bullock carts. The robed men that looked like priests were the Moors, the hired killers. They sailed away early next morning. The soldiers and slaves dug up two deep trenches, tossed in the bodies, twigs and dry wood and spilled oil from casks. As the bodies burned the two priests prayed inside the chapel after shutting its door. It seemed like they were asking for forgiveness. At their vigil through the night they were assisted by a native man. Around midnight, with the embers still glowing, the soldiers and the slaves filled up the graves. Then the priests and the native prayed over the trenches."

Just as Pedru turned to walk away, Caitu begged him to hold on.

"So how do you know what even the priests and historians don't know? And you're not even from here?"

"The story I told you was the story I heard from my great grandfather who was the 18th generation descendent of the native who did vigil with the two priests that night. The native came from the DigDhigi tribe of the Canara district. His boat had marooned on the Anjediva island. He was rescued by the soldiers and was offered work when they were building the chapel there. He became a convert long before the locals here. He came here with the priests and the soldiers. His brother back home had remained a Hindu. The cobbler who lives at the border of Bandar claims to be his Hindu descendent and the long lost cousin of mine. And mind you there was Kalia and a few native men. They were the witnesses too."

"Pedru, the priests who were slain were innocent and were not killers. They asked to be forgiven but yet they were killed. There is no proof that Hindu chiefs were buried here" Bruno countered

"Boy, neither my great grandfather nor I comment on the story though we believe it is true. Mind you, the Hindu chiefs also begged for forgiveness yet they were killed. My Hindu cousin reminds me this church is dedicated to martyrs; he insists all who die for their religion are martyrs, be they Christians, Hindus or heathens," concluded Pedru and started to walk

"The soldiers did what they were ordered to do by their commanders. What has our church to do with it? Countless have been buried over the ages. We don't know what lies buried under own houses. Let's not dig old graves Pedru," Bruno pleaded

Pedru who had already walked away shot back aloud:

"But I say all killing is evil and killing in the name of religion is a barbaric sacrilege." He hurried across the arcade and disappeared into the dungeon.

Then Caitu gave a shot:

"The drunken man has been bull-shitting."

"I don't think so Caitu; the slaying of the priests as well as the fifteen Hindu leaders is now a written history. But there is a mystery of the fort and what happened there or what they did to the dead bodies. The stories are still doing the rounds as Pedru said. But as I said let's not dig old graves, we would only go round in circles….

Caitu, its quarter to ten. Now tell me what you had to tell."

Taken aback at first, Caitu blurted out sounding casual:

"Dondu is dead, Bruno. He died of heart attack. A man from Bandar talked about it at the bar. Dondu's son found him outside his door and took him in. He was unable to walk or stand but spoke to his family. When the doctor was brought in Dondu was already dead. His son then took his body to the hospital for post mortem. That's all I heard."

Bruno's face went blank and he stuttered:

"What? Oh! Oh!..... Wait now.....Dondu is dead......And you waited this long to tell me. I could be in trouble. Dondu and his wife recognized me. For sure, Dondu has told his son that I was there. I also called out to his wife."

Unable to continue Bruno gazed over the silvery shimmer on the dark waters. Caitu shook him by the shoulder:

"So why should you be in trouble? We didn't throw him in the drain. We pulled him out and reached him to his door. You said he was a heart patient. What if he has told his family about you? The family knows you and your family."

Regaining his strength, Bruno spoke irritably:

"But you were quite rough the way you threw him up. Who knows what caused his heart attack? They will find it out at the hospital. It could also be a criminal case. The police would surely question me. I am worried how my mother will take it knowing I have to leave for Bombay shortly."

"Come on Bruno, your mother is a strong woman though she would blame me."

Bruno paced up and down the bank as loud intermittent clangs emanated from the yard nearby.

As they walked back, Caitu put his hand over Bruno's shoulder but he moved away.

"So what you think we should do now? I don't even feel like going home." Bruno's voice was plaintive.

"Let's go and watch what's left of the drama. It would help."

"Do you feel like watching the drama now? I am exhausted Caitu. Reach me home," moaned Bruno

At the graveyard Bruno broke away and peered over the wall; he saw the rectangles under the glow of the moon. He remembered the burials of his grandpa and then grandma. *'Perhaps they will come to my rescue'* he prayed quietly and caught up with Caitu who had gone past the church front. Caitu stood staring towards the gulmohar tree. There was a police jeep parked there. There was no sound of the teatro.

"That is a police jeep Caitu. What could have happened? May be there was a fight," said Bruno

Instantly, they saw Cipriano come out of the gate yelling, wagging a finger at one of the two men walking beside him; the man folded his hands as the Inspector signaled him towards the jeep. Out of earshot, the Inspector became calm and settled into a polite chat with the man. Then he sent him back and called out to his constable. They got into the jeep and it sped off from the scene.

"Something has gone wrong there. Cipriano usually comes after news of an illegal act or conduct at the drama; and that's the director he was yelling at. I thought he would take him away but he let him off," said Caitu

They were relieved to see Ronnie and Bonnie walk out of the gate.

"What are the police here for?" asked Caitu

"There was a raid after the Bombay duo João & Bobo did a spoof. It was an uncensored late addition to the program. It was very critical of Salazar," muttered Ronnie

"And how that happened? They usually get approval of the songs and the play in advance. So have they arrested the duo?" asked Caitu

"Probably the duo showed the director a false script of the spoof. They fled soon after the act. They have a name. A story is doing the round; that they had come with a plan and were paid by GFP or freedom fighters from outside. I am sure the director will be arrested. Everyone heard how Cipriano abused him and said he is going after the duo right now. The inspector is known to be tough and ruthless." Ronnie's theatrics made Caitu chuckle:

"Tough and ruthless? Ha ha… he is as corrupt as his master, the double agent under whom he works,…… and did he say he is going after the duo? He thinks they will be at their residence or with some relatives or what?"

"You should know better; you have an uncle who is a mastermind of escapes. The duo being masters of comedy must be heading to the border dressed as old women or priests." Ronnie chortled.

"Oi you, a hee-hawing hyena and a talebearer. So do you have any other news? I heard some Hindu man died at Bandar village this evening."

"How come your friend from Bandar doesn't know? We are here since early evening and still alive. I enjoyed the side show, the songs and the comedy acts. We will shoot off after the next side show, if at all the drama resumes. The play is boring; all sorrow and repentance of an alcoholic. Where did you guys disappear, to the bar?" He snickered

"This boy doesn't drink, beanpole. We went to have a look at the new bridge."

An announcement blared over the horns that the show will begin in a minute. As Caitu and Bruno walked away, there was shrill voice from behind:

"Bruno, wait," said Priscilla, the girl from his ward. "I want you to come with us after the show. We are just three of us from the ward and we don't have a torch. Will you please Bruno?" she pleaded standing a few feet away

"I don't know Priscilla, but there's moonlight so you don't need a torch. Stick to the main road until the bund road; there will be many walking along that way. You can take my torch." Bruno held out the torch to her.

"Oh no Bruno, that's alright. We will manage," she mumbled and walked away

"That girl wanted your company and not the torch. She looked hurt. May be she is in love with you," Caitu giggled back-slapping Bruno

"We had been playmates since kids. She feels safe with me. Knowing the mess we're in please don't distract me with your silly asides. I've never seen you being romantic to a girl. Tell me what you plan to do next," Bruno snapped back

"Let us walk up to the bazaar then I will ride you home," said Caitu

As they walked Caitu put his hand round Bruno's shoulder:

"I feel guilty of what I have put you through all along though the Dondu incident was not of my making. But I want you to know that I feel your pain and will stand by you," Caitu's tone had an empathic ring

Bruno response was quick:

"The way we walked away makes us guilty. We should have taken him in and called the doctor or his son. Dondu has surely told his son about me and you, the tall rowdy boy. Police will surely ask me who the other boy is. And as you are quite known to them, it will not only open your old wounds but add a new one."

"Well, I thought of a way out," Caitu retorted

"Is there a way out? The police might be at my door first thing in the morning. I don't want to miss my Africa job Caitu. I have refused two earlier offers. So what is your way out?"

"The quickest way is the illegal way. Though you planned to travel on a passport, you could be held up if there is police case. I suggest we go meet my uncle who lives in the foothills where I went two summers ago. He is a great hunter and knows all the border routes. He also knows high police officials. He now works for a mining company. I think the best thing to do is to move to his place immediately." As Caitu effused about his uncle it did little to lift up Bruno's spirits.

"The plan you're suggesting is not a good one. Those are dangerous crossings through the forests or the Ghats. There is a better and quicker route at the south. There are guides in my neighboring village. But police may be at my door first thing in the morning," Bruno grumbled

They had reached the bazaar. The shops had closed and the big moon was beaming over their tiled roofs with uniform intensity.

"You are panicking as though you are the murderer. The police would want to question you as a mere witness. But things might turn out better than you are imagining," said Caitu and picked up his bicycle. He asked Bruno to hop on the back seat.

"You expect the dead man to be alive? I don't know what to do right now. I don't even feel like going home tonight." Reacting to Bruno's plaintive tone Caitu was swift to respond:

"You don't feel like going home right now. I too feel the same. How about a little drink on our way? It will relieve our tension."

"Oh! There again; I knew you were waiting for an opportunity. But which bar would be open now? Jackinas closes by nine thirty."

"We will check; it's just minute ride on your way," quipped Caitu

Reaching the Jackinas bar Caitu put his bicycle by the pillar. The small corridor wasn't too dark with a bright moon up. On a slab below the wide latched door there lay a slouched figure. Caitu took Bruno's torch and flashed it on. A well-dressed young man was snoring away.

"That is Adolf, a young man of some education who has turned into a barfly. Right now he is doing a buzzing rondo, a finale of his concerto to his ancestors. He would be joining them soon." Caitu smothered his snigger and did a falsetto:

"Adolf, Oh Adolf; your grandpa is here. Wake up my boy. Your time hasn't come yet. Oh Adolf," uttered Caitu in croaky voice.

Adolf woke up with a jerk and a burp and stood up.

"Oh, who is it?" he said as he swayed in the dark. Going closer Caitu flashed the torch again: "Why are you still here Adolf?"

"Oh it's you Caetano. If you're going home I will come with you. Jackinas left just a while back. He closed late today; there were a few late drop-ins - shippy guys, you know. I don't know how I dropped off to sleep. I did a lot of running around, writing applications for our folks." Caitu interrupted him:

"I know. We've been pealing the bells since morning and then went for the drama. Tell me if there's a way to get a pint of some good brew somewhere and a beer for my friend? Surely you might know some toddy distiller. I heard they keep awake through the night."

"You mean the coconut toddy-tappers? Of course, they don't. In fact, they sleep early and wake up around four in the morning to fire up the distillation pot. But I can take you to Jeru's place. But sometimes she doesn't respond this late hour. We will try. Follow me; it's a ten minute walk from here."

"I will park my bicycle here and lock it," said Caitu

"Well nobody robs bicycles; they have a license, you know it," said Adolf

The three then walked along a sand path that first meandered round a few large houses; dogs barked from some balconies and a couple of them around the courtyards charged at them. As Adolf gave a shout they stayed away but still barked.

"These pariah-dogs bark but don't bite. Actually they're not barking at me but at you. I often throw some bread or left-over crumbs. Well, some guys I know prefer Jeru's place because it's quiet and cozy; but it's late now," he jabbered on

The houses became sparse and smaller in size and their sand path turned narrow and shadowy under tall fruit trees; the path headed across a bund through the fields.

"Are we crossing that bund; it's a long way off Adolf. I can see that you're also a bit wobbly now. You surely had one too many," Caitu snorted

"No Caetano, we have reached. There's a little cottage to your right at the edge of the field. It is not visible from here because of the bushy hedge. Follow behind me with your torch on. Snakes often prop up, some so thin you can't see them under moonlight," said Adolf

Going round the hedge, Adolf led them into an open area of dried scrub, then over a sandy patch, onto a little mud cottage. They climbed the two steps and were in the small verandah. The boys sat on the two cement seats as Adolf knocked on the door. Getting no response he knocked again calling out aloud:

"Jeru! Oh Jeru!" A hoarse sleepy voice of a woman responded after a while. "Who is it?"

"It's me Adolf, Jeru,"

"Adolf, I am not opening the door for you. Is this the time for you to disturb me from my sleep for your drink? Often you don't even have the money to pay. I am sleeping now. Go home," she shouted

"No Jeru. It is not for me. There are two boys here, very decent boys," said Adolf

"Oh! Decent boys who loaf about at midnight," she croaked

"It's not yet midnight. It's about quarter to eleven. And they are ready to pay whatever your price and more."

Caitu felt he should second him: "Auntie Jeru, give us just one pint of feni and a beer if you have and we will pay whatever your charges."

His interjection worked; she kept grumbling but finally the door creaked opened. A frail middle-aged woman appeared at the doorway.

"Adolf, you are on the road to ruin. You drink through day and night. After all your education, you have turned into an alcoholic. People say it's because of some girl. God will punish me for serving you a drink. Every time I tell myself I must stop it. Can't you find a job for yourself?"

"No Jeru, I am doing a bit on the side, writing applications for our ignorant folks like you. Have I not done your applications? That I drink a bit more is God's wish. Forgive me! But they say Jesus drank wine with his disciples." He smothered chuckle.

"You rascal, you are already drunk. You are cursing yourself by such mockery," she wailed

The lady turned to the boys: "I hear enough sermons in the church; I don't want a drunken man's blasphemy here. It's late in the night. You seem too young to drink. What do you want anyway?"

"We are not young, auntie. We are adults and are out of school, I mean finished our school. Now, get us a pint of feni and a beer and two glasses."

"I don't have a beer. I just finished my lime cordial. I have Vimto if you like. I keep it because my nephew likes it," she retorted

"I don't mind anything to make it lighter and sweeter. But let me see how much I've got in my pocket." As Bruno tried to check his pocket, Caitu pushed him aside:

"Stop it Bruno. I will pay for everything," he retorted and turned to Jeru again:

"Now, make it two pints and three glasses. I forgot about Adolf. He must be duly compensated for bringing us here. We will guzzle it down quick; give us ten minutes. And give us some lime cordial with two sodas. Feni is strong stuff for my friend here; he will have it with Vimto."

Jeru went in and did three return trips placing their order on the bench.

They poured their drinks in the glasses and came out and sat on the sands under the open sky while the woman sat in the verandah with a lamp next to her. As they imbibed the country spirit the fears and trepidation that haunted them began to evaporate. Things now didn't look as bad as they did a few minutes ago. Bruno looked up at the moon and felt it smiled at him. Caitu indulged in some banter with Adolf at times turning boisterous.

Then Jeru started beaming signals, a yawn or a bout of cough.

After a while she told them to hurry up: "You said ten minutes but its twenty minutes now," she grumbled

Caitu tried to pour a little from the pint into Bruno's glass.

"No Caitu. I am not used to this hard stuff. I will be sick," he protested

"A few droplets Bruno; they will give you solace. Look, how Adolf is beaming like the moon above," enthused Caitu

"Eternal solace! I do need it," exclaimed Adolf with a twist of his tongue

This time Jeru gave them a shout asking to wind up.

Bruno got up: "Let's go Caitu. If you can't finish the pint throw it out and return the pint," he said and hurried to the verandah

Emptying a larger portion in his own glass Caitu handed the pint to Adolf who gulped down the remnants with effort. Caitu rushed in as Bruno tried pay.

"How much is it Auntie Jeru?" he asked

"Two rupias for the two pints and one rupia and two annas for the soda and the Vimto. You can pay me three rupias," she said. Caitu gave the woman four rupias and she seemed more than content.

She waited to see them off and went in after they had hobbled over the hedge. Once across it, while Caitu and Bruno walked on springy legs, Adolf dragged behind unsteadily making the boys wait. Then he moved under a tree and began to pee prompting the boys to follow suit.

"Adolf Hitler, you're unable to lead us. Looks like you've had one too many before we met you," yelled Caitu

"No, Caitu, I am not out yet. Yes, I had drink at Jackinas; a man named Raghu offered me a half pint. I had done applications for him. He came in late and wanted a drink because his uncle had died at Bandar and he was sad for it." Adolf's speech was slurring.

A bell rang for the boys.

"Did he tell you the dead man's name or other names Adolf?" asked Caitu

"He said some names but I don't remember. Raghu said the old man had gone out in his backyard suspecting someone was cutting off his banana bunch. He caught two men in the act but seeing him they fled and he got pushed in the drain.

Then two boys rushed there; one, a villager known to him and the other, a tall boy.... who threw the man up from the drain ....and he got sick. They left him near door and walked away. His son found him near the......banana tree........ The man spoke to his family.... also told some names ....but later died," Adolf murmured with pauses

Stunned into silence, the boys exchanged quick furtive glances. Bruno nudged Caitu with his elbow.

Caitu suddenly turned round and caught Adolf's neck and started pressing it: "You're drunk and yet can remember the whole story but not any names? Did the man tell any names," he yelled

Bruno grabbed Caitu from behind and pulled him away.

"Don't worry, I was not killing him," he snapped

Regaining his composure Caitu watched Adolf sway as he stood with his feet apart. Caitu took a step back and put his arm around him.

"Caetano! Why don't you kill me? I often feel it is time for me to go," he said without emotion

"I wasn't killing you. And you're not going anywhere. You are done with your studies and you still feel you have a problem. Then what should I feel? Now tell me did Raghu give any names? Did he say who threw the old man up?"

"Well, I remember a bit. Raghu said his uncle's name was Dond… one robber was Salador and one of the two boys who came next was….. Brun." Adolf paused, "May be it was Brun who threw him up….. Then, a fracas broke out on the next table. Raghu got disturbed. I mean he was already disturbed. Before he left he asked me to have a peg."

Caitu yelled at him: "You don't know what you're talking. You're giving your own names. Couldn't you ask him properly? How do you manage to write applications for clients, you educated drunken ass."

"I usually don't poke my nose in when guys chat in the bar. I sit in a corner or outside. Raghu asked me to sit with him and started talking. Also, Caitu I don't write applications when I am drunk. And why am I telling you all this. Oh yes, because you asked me if I had drinks in the bar," said Adolf

"Cool guy, that's a flash of clarity even when you are so drunk. Any particular reason then, why you began drinking Adolf?" asked Bruno

"Forget it. Don't know myself. Let's go home now," he muttered

Reaching Jackinas bar, they watched Adolf stagger and slump at the same spot he was earlier. He now moaned with emotional pauses:

"When I go home late and drunk....they make hell of a noise..... father opens door... ...stares and then shuts the door. Right now.... . feeling more tired ... sleepy than drunk. Will sleep for an hour and then go."

"You stay just there Adolf and I will pick you up on my way back."

Caitu caught hold of his bicycle and said: "Bruno, let's walk a while as we plan our move."

The main road was deserted. Moonlight streamed through gaps and slits in the foliage of the trees. As Bruno walked with his head down he saw on the mud road a mosaic in motion of moon shadows and streaks of ochre and leaden spots. He thought they had gone with Adolf to drown a bad memory but he had refreshed it with add-ons of his own.

"Dondu is dead but surely he has tagged me with you lurking behind. Adolf uttered my name saying I threw him up from the trench. I know he didn't mean it. I feel sorry for him," said Bruno

"Don't get swayed by his drunken babble. It has no significance. Dondu is a friend of your family. So when he asked if you would stand witness against a robber, he asked you a favor; you told him no. And it is not even a robbery, just backyard break-in."

"But it's not only of being a witness against someone I don't know. The more serious issue is what caused Dondu's heart attack. Before you threw him up from the trench Dondu was fine," Bruno's tone had a woeful ring

"You mean to say I caused his heart attack. I had caught him firmly so he would not slip down; it's quite a deep drain."

"So, what should we do now? What are we going to say if we are called by the police? They may even question us separately. You may tell lies that I wouldn't know of. Also, I am not comfortable telling lies," said Bruno

"So you would tell them I was rough with the old man. I have no problem Bruno. I care about you more than about myself."

Alerted by the blaring horn of an approaching truck they stepped aside to safety as it trundled down with a load of bare-chested men.

"Any idea as to who these men might be? Could be convicts being shifted to Agonda jail," muttered Caitu

"We might be the next on our way there. Don't you belittle the poor hard-working men? They are the workers who are building our bridge," Bruno turned to look back

"People are returning home after the drama. Get on your bicycle and reach me to the end of our bund road but only if you can, but go slow. You also drank a lot. As much as I am terribly shaken I feel exhausted. And that little drink is still reeling my head," muttered Bruno

"I am perfectly fine to ride you. Come sit on the bar," said Caitu and pedaled off with extra caution as he kept on talking:

"Pluck up courage boy! We can handle it even in the worst case. You have finished school and had planned to go to Bombay or Africa. I had long been on papa's notice and have now quit school. Though papa has given up on me, I could use a few of his contacts that could give me a break. I could seek my step-brother's help too. So let's get out of here together; forget the hassle of travel documents. As I told you, let's go to my uncle's place tomorrow itself."

"So we go there and your uncle takes us across the border? Which border crossing and how do we proceed to Bombay from there? I have to convince my mother."

"Listen, we go there first and tell him of our problem. He would find a way out. He has influence with the police. He is straight and honest. If he cannot do it he would tell us. But in case he needs a day more, we could wait. So, I suggest we go in the morning and if there is no firm answer from him we return home by evening and take the southern route.

You pack a few clothes, like shorts, trousers, vests and a towel; also a few important certificates – well you know what not. You meet me at Kunkali at 09:15 tomorrow at the Kepem junction. Don't wait at the first bus-stop? You know just opposite is the police station. I will be in the Kepem *carreira*."

They had reached the end of the bund road. Bruno told Caitu to stop and he got off the bicycle. He stood aside and blurted out:

"You said your uncle is a hunter and now working in the mines. Reaching there, we might find him busy at the mines or gone on some hunting trip."

"You're mistaken Bruno. Mama told me he made great sacrifices for his family and even for friends. He would find a way for us. Moreover, at his house we would be in safe territory. Think about it. If you're ready for it tell me now as it's getting late and we both need to sleep." There was ring of finality the way Caitu turned around the bicycle, moving a few yards away.

"Just wait." Bruno mumbled: "What should I do?" he paused, "Alright! I will be there at Kunkali tomorrow morning. But what do I tell my mother when she sees me now? I never went home this late and drunk like this," Bruno mumbled grumpily

"You hardly drank anything Bruno. Now, let me think what you must say.... . Oh yes, tell her we were invited at my friend's house. My neighbors have just come down from Nairobi for a vacation. I was there for their son's birthday. The only thing is, you weren't there and it was yesterday. But I will vouch for you, if your mother asks," Caitu tried to laugh it off

"I won't do that. Tell me, do you always lie to your mother? I try not to and at times when I do I end up suffocating myself for days. Often I get caught. She reads my face as I speak. I don't know how she does it. Now, tell me your uncle's village. You only told me it's in the foothills; there are scores of hamlets around the Ghats. Mother won't let me leave the house without knowing where exactly I am going."

"Oh! Mama's tenderhearted boy, come out of it. Everybody tells lies here and there. Young and old or wise and the fools do. Our parents hide many things from us. Well, the name let me remember..." he cocked his one eye skywards at the moon that had dipped in the northwest sky.

"Tell me your uncle's name and address Caitu," Bruno yelled back

"My uncle lives in a hamlet of Adnem, a side stream you are familiar with. The small ward is cut off from the larger village of Rivna. His name I had told you when you came home. He is 'caçador Alexandre', alias 'caçador Alês', that is, 'Alex the hunter' - a great hunter as I told you," Caitu enthused aloud, his voice echoing over the Bandar lake

"Great hunter eh! Now go and pick up Adolf, if he's still around. But see that you guys don't fall off into the fields," Bruno yelled, waving out till Caitu shot out of sight.

When he knocked his mother was swift to open the door. A burning lamp lay on the floor below the armchair. As the boy walked by, she sniffed frowning at him:

"Bruno! You smell foul, of strong drink. Your face and eyes are red. What is it? Can you explain to me?" she gasped

"Mãe, I am quite tired and want to sleep. I will speak to you in the morning," he mumbled

"But it's already 12 AM. in the morning. Tell me what happened?" she asked

He headed straight to the dining table, gulped down a mug of water and came back to his room, changed and got into his bed. Mother stood in the doorway with the lamp in hand. When he turned round to face the wall, she quietly moved away.

The events of the evening streamed into Bruno's head causing confusion and restlessness. But the physical exhaustion and the effect of alcohol sedated him and he fell into a deep slumber.

At six thirty in the morning Ana heard repeated knocking at the backdoor. Even before she could reach the door she heard a low muttering voice: "Ana, Oh Ana, are you there? It's me Matil."

As Ana unlatched the door Matil pushed in, pulling Ana along into the dining room. When they had sat down at the table she began in a subdued tone:

"Is Bruno awake? He might be wanted for questioning by the police. And he was to travel to Africa. But he might be held up now."

"Bruno is still sleeping. He came very late last night. The police want to question him about what Matil?" Words dribbled down Ana's half-open mouth.

"Ana, please don't panic. Just know I am there for you as always. Goldsmith Dondu died last night of a heart attack. Around seven-thirty he came out into his backyard and caught two men cutting away a banana bunch from his plantation. As they fled in panic Dondu got pushed into a rain-drain. Then Bruno appeared there with a tall boy. They pulled Dondu up and left him at his door and walked away."

"I got it. Bruno came from the chapel with Caetano around eight and they left for the teatro," said Ana in a tremulous voice

"Well the incident could have happened before that. The boys could have gone there hearing Dondu's shouts.

He is a frail man with a loud voice," said Matil

"That means they went to his help and he was alive and well when they left. How and when he died?"

"Dondu's son found him by the back door, quite ill. He spoke to his son and wife before he got worse. He mentioned two names, Salvador as one of the robbers and Bruno as the witness. He died before the doctor was brought in. Later at the hospital the doctors said it was a heart attack. This is what I heard from Dondu's neighbor," Matil paused

"So what Bruno has to do with his death and why Dondu put Bruno as a witness and not Caetano?" asked Ana

"Dondu doesn't know Caetano. He talked about him as the tall boy who pushed him up the drain in anger because he had mistaken him to be one of the robbers. He saw Bruno later."

"Oh, I got it. Bruno has been in all kinds of trouble ever since he met this boy. To keep him away from him Roque sent him off to Belgaum. And when things seemed to be going well, now this happened. Bruno was expecting his travel documents in a week's time and then travel to Africa. It might not happen now. I don't know what to do."

Holding her face in her palms, Ana dipped her head on the table and sobbed quietly for a minute. Then she steadied herself.

Standing behind, pouring words of comfort the gentle hands of Matilda pressed the shoulders of her bosom friend. She tried to do her own analysis:

"Bruno hasn't done anything. Dondu's wife or son will never accuse him. They always spoke well of you as a family. But Dondu was taken to the hospital after he died. There was an incident before Dondu's death. So the police have to investigate: collect doctor's opinion and evidence from Dondu's family, and the spot of the incident. The case has to close leaving no doubt," Matil paused to take a breath

"I am really tired of all this. Bruno could miss a good job in Africa," moaned Ana

"Ana, things could have been worse. I think Bruno should cooperate with the police and clear his name. He might miss one job but will get opportunities because he is intelligent, hard-working and honest. Better still, he could do college. But if you feel he shouldn't miss his Africa job, we can send him the illegal way. There are guides in our neighboring village who take people across the southern border. Let us wait till the end of this day. Wake him up now and explain to him. I will be back by afternoon. If the police come asking for him, tell them he is out but will report to them as soon as he comes. I can keep him with my brother or even my cousin's house for a couple of days." Matil hugged Ana and walked out by the back door.

CHAPTER XXV

Knocks at the Door-The Getaway

Bruno was nearly awake as he heard a knock: "Wake up Bruno, there's someone knocking at the front door." He turned and saw his mother at the door. As she went away he dozed off when he heard more knocks:

"Wake up Bruno, there's man named Adolf. When I didn't open the door he came in by the back door. He says Inspector Cipriano and two constables are sitting in the verandah and they have handcuffs with them. What did you do Bruno?" Get up Bruno!" Ana wailed and walked away from the door as Adolf barged in

"You shameless man, why did you come into my room? A man who seemed decent and humble, is an informer? I even reminded Caitu to take you home," Bruno shouted as he sat on the bed

Adolf laughed and then calmed down:

"That was nice of you. Caitu took me home alright; he also told me you two went to Dondu's help and he threw Dondu up in anger and he got a heart attack. He then begged me to save him as he knew you will give witness against him because you have more sympathy for Dondu. I asked how I could help him. He said I must tell the police that I was there and saw you throw Dondu up saying: *'Dondu is dying so let's kill him anyway'.* I agreed because Caitu is my childhood friend. This morning we met the Inspector and I testified ...... So Bruno the Inspector knows you caused Dondu's heart attack. He is at your door with two constables. Get up. You have hurt your mother too. Now, don't pretend you're falling asleep Bruno. Bruno!"

"Caitu and you! Traitors! You get out of my house?" Bruno screamed as he got up and lunged at Adolf and grabbed his neck. As he kept pressing, Adolf slipped slipped out of his grip and ran out of the room. Bruno's hands felt the cold wall even as he heard his name being called out again.

"Bruno, get up now!" The voice had a familiar ring and he felt a hand on his back. Awake, he turned round but didn't open his eyes as it dawned on him that the reality would be worse than the lucid persecutory dream he had just woken up from.

When he did open his eyes he saw his mother staring down at him. He couldn't tell if it was a look of dejection or fury. He glanced towards the window as a shaft of light pierced through a crack quivering his vision. When he looked at her again her eyes had moistened and the remnants of the night's drinking bout evaporated. He couldn't find a voice or words to speak. He pulled out his Romer watch from under the pillow and tried wind it ever so slowly.

Ana ordered him to sit up as she broke the silence:

"Do you have an explanation for what happened last evening and the lies you told me? Have you any idea what disgrace you brought to yourself and your family?"

"What lies are you talking of mãe?" he asked

"Matilda came in with the news that Dondu is dead and that you and Caetano went to rob his bananas and pushed him into the drain and ran away. You could be charged for murder." Her tone was harsh and blunt

Her lips quivered seeing her son cringe. *'I may have hit him too hard, I shouldn't have been so blunt'* she thought. She waited with anxiety for his response.

Though fully awake and sober now, Bruno felt a throb in his belly and the temples. He was thirsty too. The discomfort perhaps dulled the impact of his mother's charge, though he sensed she was adding her own to it. In a way it was a relief to hear that she already knew it. But a tear of anguish in her eyes melted him too. He felt more comfortable with an angry mother who dealt with him harshly, which was quite hard for her to do.

He walked to the window and opened it. He saw the sun-rays weave a tapestry of dancing lights through the moistened foliage. He took a deep breath and exhaled it and felt it was smelly. He opened the second window and saw the two bunds cutting through the fields; the bund path that joined the sub-wards and the bund road that met the high bund road to Kunkali. He had seen the time on his watch was past eight. Caitu had told him to reach Kunkali by 09:15. His mother sat there waiting for his response.

"We are not the robbers, mãe. We saw two miscreants run away. We went to Dondu's help hearing his cries; we found him in the drain. Dondu asked me to give witness. I will tell you. But let me have a quick wash. Give me something to eat. I am in hurry to leave."

Ana gave him a stare. Then she became frantic:

"Leave to where? You're not going anywhere. Tell me the truth or let me take you to the police before they come to my house."

Many of Bruno's firsts were with his mother: from the day of birth, to first day at school, to the sacraments of Holy Communion and Confirmation. The only time he remembered his father when he had taken him for a movie at the church and then to meet Prof. Leitão.

Through his childhood, mother and grandmother infused in him a strong dose of religiosity, invoking tales of God's retribution against disobeying God's laws, committing a crime or lying to parents. Retribution was the Eternal fire of Hell. But he was long past his childhood and it was his mother's anguish that moved him.

Ana pulled Bruno by the hand and led him into the entrance near the little altar. A book lay on the table:

"You have lied since yesterday. Folks in the village know the whole story. When you came home from the chapel last night the incident had already happened but you didn't tell me. Now put your hand here, look up and tell me the whole truth."

The firmness of her tone put Bruno at ease. He told her the whole story in haste and felt relieved. She had calmed down by now.

"You should have put him in his house or taken him to the doctor, knowing his son wasn't there. If you had told me then, I would have gone to his house immediately. You know how much he respected your father?" She shook her head

"But mãe, he sat there as if didn't want to go in. The door was open. He seemed a bit short of breath but I never thought he would die."

"So what now, the police will look to question you."

"Yes they would. I could wait and clear my name. But I don't want to miss the Africa job. Caetano is taking me to his uncle who lives in the Sanguem foothills. He is a hunter and knows all the border crossings. He also knows top police officers." Bruno hurried into his room and began sifting through his things on his study table.

Ana followed behind but didn't interfere with what he was doing.

"And now you want to go again with this loafer who drinks and tells you to drink too? Have you not had enough of him?" she asked

"He didn't tell me to drink. You know I don't drink. I was beside myself when I heard that Dondu died. But now there is no other way. We have to leave together, illegally." His tone was firm

"So what good would it do to go to the foothills? And if the police ask for you what should I say. Matilda said she could keep you with her brother in the harbor town or with her cousin's in the north."

"Mãe, harbor town is full of police. North is too far with river crossings. Caetano says his uncle's place is safe. The nearest police station is miles away. The journey will take only three *carreiras*; we catch the first one at 9:30 at Kunkali bazaar. That is, after a while from now," he muttered seemingly restless

"Which foothill of Sanguem? The village doesn't have a name? Give me the exact place, the village, the ward and the man's name. Otherwise I won't let you go."

Unable to recall the name, he gave a wayward reply:

"For the address, you may please go to Caetano's house and ask his mother. Mãe, let me hurry please. There's really no time. Give me something to eat and a coffee please," he blurted out and walked away before she could respond

Bruno was swift with his morning chores. Pushing his things into a shoulder bag, he scrambled to the dining table. His mother served him an omelet, bread and a mug of coffee. Then she went back and brought him a tiffin box and a bottle of water:

"Put these in your bag," she said sitting beside him

"But I won't go to Caetano's house. Were you so reckless not to ask his uncle's name and address? And leave me in nerve-racking tension and face the neighbors, the village and the police? I know otherwise you're so organized. Are you under Caetano's magic spell or what?"

she wailed

Her wail spurred his memory: *'Caetano had mentioned Sal river – the side river- Oh yes'*

"I got it mãe; he lives in the ward of Rivna village called Adnem. His name is Alexandre. They call him caçador Alês or Alex the hunter. He knows many travel guides and the routes to get across the borders." He beamed as though fired by renewed energy

"Don't you get carried away with that boy's boasts? Guides you said, and those passes through the Ghats? We have heard of travelers being mauled or killed by a tiger and even robbed by the guides who take them," she kept whining as her son responded:

"We are going to find out first. His uncle now works for a mining company and knows high police officials. So he could also help in the police case. And mãe, I will not go without saying good bye to you. I will be back in a day."

That seemed to calm her nerves.

Despite the stress within, Bruno tried to stay composed for his mother's sake.

"Mãe, don't bother about what people say. Keep calm and don't answer any queries about me. Say I am fine and have gone to meet a friend. If police ask for me, tell them you will bring me to them the moment I am back."

Mother was astonished and yet relieved by her son's calm tone.

After saying a short prayer, she gave him an emotional hug moaning as she did. Soon, with a bag over his shoulder Bruno walked off quietly by the front door. He hurried down the sandy bund path and midway crossed the field and climbed the bund road that met the high bund road to Kunkali.

CHAPTER XXVI

Alone Again

There was no news of Matilda throughout the day and a few visitors who dropped in at Ana's house and the neighbors she met near the well only made random comments: *'Dondu died of heart attack,'* said one; *'Dondu fell in the drain and died,'* said another

At four in the afternoon she headed to the chapel. As she passed by a few houses, women from their backyards greeted Ana. Their somber faces and suggestive remarks or queries made her uneasy:

The first one asked: *'is the story we're hearing true Ana?'* The second one was more sympathetic: *'Oh it cannot be true Ana, everyone knows what Bruno is...'.* Ana kept her composure remembering Bruno's words.

The last man she passed by was Tonto who spoke aloud: *'Ana, Dondu was found dead by the banana tree; the banana tree killed him because he would tie a bell round its kiddies' neck and then put them on lottery. He also made stories about me saying I am robbing his bananas.'*

Tonto burst into a hollow contemptuous laugh, wished Ana a good evening and sprinted off.

Ana met the chaplain at his residence.

"Ana, what is the matter, you look worried," he asked

Ana recounted the Dondu story as told by her son and Matilda. The chaplain remained composed as he spoke:

"This Caetano is a problem child, though talented. Bruno told me he is affected by a family tragedy and needed help. I feel he needs medical help more than anything. Imagine, he served at the church and then went to a seminary school. He rebelled against his papa. A priest from his church told me the boy was influenced by an uncle who is a freedom fighter and a communist. When he came here and played the banjo, he seemed like an angel. I had prayed over him. I don't know how Bruno got attached to him at his own risk.

Now that you told me what happened, the police will certainly investigate even if it is a minor offence as the victim died later. The boys are witnesses. Bruno will have to stick around till he is cleared. Now Ana, the only succor I can give you is by prayer," concluded the chaplain

"But Father I have just two more questions: Should I seek Prof. Leitão's help? Secondly, is it right for Bruno to leave the territory by illegal route?"

"Ana, you don't know yet of the nature of the complaint. So wait for a day. Second, if things get worse let him go illegally. What is termed illegal by man's law could be just in the eyes of God. He is innocent; let him go whichever way available.

Now let me pray over you as you stand there." He placed his right hand on her head and prayed for a minute and concluded: "Go home in peace and keep calling the

Lord's name every time you are disturbed."

Ana came home and locked herself for rest of the day. Long after the Angelus bell, she took a torch and went out again. *'I might as well go and visit Dondu's house. It might help clear the air. They always spoke well of us.'*

As she approached Dondu's back door, through the grill window she saw movement of people and heard loud voices of men. She retreated towards the banana plantation. Flashing her torch, she saw the banana bunch Bruno had described. It lay there broken and hanging with two ripened bananas. A chill rippled through her body. She turned to go home.

She approached her house with a tinge of sadness as it lay in darkness within, while its gabled roof and the verandah were bathed in gold dust. The moon had just risen. She unlocked the padlock, got in and latched her back door.

She quickly lit a couple of chimney lamps; she put one on the dining table, and walked with the other into her bedroom and sat at a corner table and thought for a moment. From the drawer she pulled out a letter pad and set to write to Roque. Wayward thoughts entered her head. *'What am I going to write? There is nothing to write; Roque always blamed me whenever Bruno faltered: that I always wanted him in my custody though I couldn't handle him. Was I using Bruno to fill my own emptiness arising out of my husband's long absences? Was I so possessive so as to ruin his future?'*

Overcome with emotion her thoughts diverted to her son. It was the first time he wasn't at home since he had returned from Belgaum. She wondered what he must be doing in the remote foothills with Caetano. *'He could be the Satan who has now taken Bruno to his den.'*

Beside herself, she ran near the wall and started banging her head: *'Get these thoughts out, my God. I am going mad here.'* She winced in pain as the rugged stone stung her forehead. Remembering what the chaplain had said, she recited the Lord's name.

She lay down on her bed till the pain subsided. In a corner there was a metal trunk sitting on top of another larger trunk. Digging her hand inside the top trunk she pulled out a bunch of keys. With one of the keys she opened her wardrobe door and with another she opened a drawer. She frisked through knick-knack of chains, curios and coins and pulled out a little silver box. Carrying it to the side table, she opened the box and scrutinized its contents: there were over a dozen coins known locally as *sarvonnas,* the 7-8 gram 22-carat imitations ofthe British sovereign. She picked out eight and put them in an envelope and put the silver box back in the drawer.

Then she ate a little and went to bed. She lay awake for two long hours turning and twisting until the exhaustion took over and put her to sleep.The shrill crowing of the rooster in the coop woke her up as usual at five. She knew there wasn't much to do, Bruno being away. She finished a few things that were left undone, fed the fowls and the pigs. When she was done, she didn't know what to do.

She went into her son's room and lay down on his bed. She felt better and slowly fell off to sleep again.

She was woken up by a hard knocking at the door. She got up and hurried into the entrance. It was past nine on the clock. *'My God, have I ever slumbered like this, and with all the misery around?'*

When she opened the door she was terrified to see two policemen, a Portuguese *cabo* and a native constable.

"Bom dia Senhora," said the *cabo*

"Bom dia senhor," she replied in a tremulous voice

Cabo turned to the assistant: *"Conte a ela sobre o aviso do filho dela,"* he said firmly and plumped on the verandah recliner. The constable gave Ana a nod and assumed a serious posture as he spoke:

"Are you the mother of Bruno Coelho?"

"Yes, *senhor,* please come and seat inside and be comfortable. Have some tea please," she pleaded

He told her not to worry and spoke again:

"There is summons for Bruno as a witness though he's not been accused of any offence. Is he in the house? If so, can you tell him to come out?"

"No *senhor*, Bruno is not in the house. He went out saying he would be back by evening. He said he is going to meet a friend. But witness to what?" she asked politely

The constable narrated the incident as told by Dondu's son at the Kunkali police station. Ana felt it was similar to her son's account.

"Bruno did speak to me about it. But my son hasn't done anything. Why do you want him *senhor*?"

"There was death and a complaint thereafter. The man has given two names, Salvador the robber and Bruno, the witness. Salvador is not traceable. But we need your son to begin the enquiry though his family has no complaints against him. Dondu named Bruno as the witness who saw the two offenders flee."

"But my son told me he doesn't know them. Also, he doesn't want to get tied down in a police case as he has to leave soon for a job," she pleaded

"We know your son is not the accused. We want to know from him what all happened. We want to know who the tall boy is who was with him. We have to move forward with the enquiry. Then he is free but cannot leave the territory till the case is closed."

"So how many days it will take to close the case?" she asked

"Cannot say for now; may be a week or a month," he said curtly

The *cabo* who sat listening seemed restless. He got up as he called out to his assistant: *"Avise-a e leve sua assinatura; vamos."* Then he went down the steps and lit a cigarette.

The constable moved to the side bench and held out a duplicate booklet for Ana to sign. Tearing off a page, he gave it to her. He spoke a little firmly this time:

"This is a copy of the preliminary police intimation to Bruno. We are waiting for him and his companion. If Bruno doesn't report by tomorrow, we will issue a warrant to search and bring him in."

The discourse which the officer had begun with due moderation had ended in a veiled threat. With trepidation Ana watched them leave by the back of her house.

The sight of police walking through the village raised curious eyebrows and murmurs and served as fine grist for the gossip-mill to excite a dull evening. Ana, herself being a product of rustic upbringing, felt conscious and ashamed. Whilst the constable was speaking to her, Ana had an eye on the neighbor's house which stood a hundred yards apart. She had seen the lady leaning over the window, seemingly, dusting off a pillow, a doormat and then a linen piece. Lately they weren't on speaking terms.

Ana bolted the front and the back door. Her windows were not yet opened. Sitting at a table in her bedroom, she tried to make calculations on a letter pad. A sovereign, she knew, was worth about 20 rupias but across the borders, she had heard, it was twice or thrice the value. *'How much should I put aside for Bruno? I am sure Matil would know it better,'* she thought

Late afternoon Matilda showed up and Ana told her of the policemen's visit.

"I know about it Ana. They had parked their jeep near the cross. It is quite a long way to walk from there. A few tongues started wagging as I came in. Now tell me what exactly they said to you, nothing more. Leave your comments later."

After hearing Ana she responded:

"I had been to Dondu's house and met his wife this afternoon. Dondu was consigned to the flames by the bank of Adnem. I am told his ashes will be taken to the Shanta Durga temple to ensure that the journey of his soul is hassle-free. The ashes will then be brought back and immersed in the river or in the sea."

Matil paused seeing Ana twitching her lips.

"Look Ana, Dondu has spoken to his family naming Bruno as witness and Salvador, the accused. The victim is now cremated. Dondu's son told me he has no ill-will towards Bruno or his family. Yet he wants the two main culprits arrested though the police suspect they have fled. He also wants to know who the tall boy is who was rough with his father. And only Bruno can tell who that boy is." As Matil concluded Ana fumed:

"That Caetano has taken my son into every hole he has gone into. So what should Bruno do now? He doesn't want to miss his job. He has an old passport. He was waiting for his new travel documents."

"It's best that Bruno and that rascal to move out of here. As things are now, the illegal way is the only way," said Matil

"Why should Caetano go with Bruno? Let him fend for himself?" said Ana irritably

"Two reasons. First, it is a big risk if he stays behind here. He is also a tough guy," rejoined Matil

"Matil, who to approach then?"

"My neighbor, *Tai* spoke of Diggu, the cobbler who lives on the edge of our village. He is a Canara native who journeys through southern border. Though there have been complaints about him by women, the boys need not worry about it. His fees are reasonable. *Tai* said it is safer to go through Kishu who uses Diggu at short notice and has control over him. Well, you know Kishu, the freedom fighter from Tulsi village. *Tai* will get me the news by evening. But your son isn't here yet. Did he tell you when he will be back?"

"He should be back by evening. He went with Caetano to his uncle's house. He lives in the foothills of Rivna. Caetano told him his uncle is a great hunter who knows all border crossings. He also knows police officers." Matil put her hand up:

"Oh, he went with that devil again! But don't you talk about those Ghats Ana. In the forests there are wild animals, pythons and cobras. Then there are rivers and streams to cross where crocodiles hide. My brother knows it all. Even as a guard, he only scouts around the boundary," Matil whined

Ana was thrown off-guard again, and was wringing her hands in helplessness.

"Come on Ana, what is wrong with you. Don't worry about it. I will see that Bruno crosses the borders safely. But it's all stuffy here. Why have you shut the windows?" As Matil turned to unlatch it, Ana caught her hand:

"Let it be Matil, let's go and sit in my bedroom. The window is open there," she said. When they had sat down on the bed, Ana spoke:

"I don't want to talk to anyone, not even neighbors fearing they might enquire about Bruno and then I wouldn't know what to say. Not that we fight like our old women used to. We don't." Ana's snigger made Matil burst into a laugh.

"Ana, you're being distracted here. Let's concentrate on Bruno. Now he should have money with him to last the journey till he reaches a safe place like Belgaum or Bombay. You cannot give him all Portuguese rupias. Once he crosses the borders, the rupias have little value. Do you have *sarvonnas*?"

"I have kept aside eight pieces. How many you think should he carry with him and how? We've heard of robberies," said Ana

"It's risky for women and children without a man. But they are big boys and with that devil Caetano you need not worry. He mustn't exchange all coins within the territory. Let him hide five in his inner garment; make two secret pockets and put a few stitches. The other three let him carry safely in his trouser pocket, but also stitched. Give him rupias for the way." Matil got up and moved towards the bedroom door.

"Got it Matil. I did it once when he went back after his last vacation."

"I am going now Ana. If Bruno comes back this evening you could send him to my place if needed."

"Hold on Matil," said Ana, as she paced up to her and mumbled: "my bosom friend and an angel." She gave Matil a long tight hug and pecked her on the cheek and on the neck.
"Come sit with me for a while and have some tea and biscuits," she whimpered

"Leave it for now Ana, we will sit together for long chats after Bruno has crossed to safety. We could have some wine too," Matil tittered as she walked out.

Glossary

- *Agente* – a police officer
- *Ah merda….este bastardo…é um mentiroso* -Oh shit….this bastard is a liar
- *Avise-a e leve sua assinatura; vamos* – give her the notice and take her signature; let's go.
- *Bom dia senhora/senhor* – Good morning madam/sir
- *Cabo* - a corporal, a police inspector or officer
- *Comunidade* – A local community with collective ownership of land-holdings
- *Conte a ela sobre o aviso do filho dela* – Tell her about her son's notice
- *Fado:* a popular iconic Portuguese song performed by a *Fadisto/a* (a male or female vocalist) accompanied by two guitars (a Portuguese and a classical type)
- *Guarda*: a guard or a constable
- *Levante-o! Vamos interrogar esse vagabundo* – Pick him up; let's interrogate this bum
- *Mãe – (Portuguese /Konkani)* -mother
- *Polícia Secreta* – Secret Police, Criminal Police
- *Quem está dentro ái …sai..sai apresse* – whoever is inside, get out quickly
- **Regidor/regedor** – a government appointed village head to settle disputes during the Portuguese rule in Goa

- *Rupia* – a Portuguese rupee (*compare:* Indian rupiah)
- *Vai , vai embora, vai todos para casa* – go, go away, go home everybody
- *Venha aqui, apresse* - come here quick

KONKANI (Goan language):

- *Ayi –or – Aee* (Konkani/Marathi) – A Hindu mother
- *Bebinca –* **or** *bibik* (Portuguese/Konkani) a popular delicious multi-layered Goan cake/sweet with soft rubbery feel (made with flour, sugar, ghee, egg yolk & coconut milk)
- *Bhag or bhagai – an orchard* of fruit trees or palms
- *Bavú* **or** *Baú-* used to address a brother /friend
- *Dekhni or Mando,-* two styles of Goan folk dance song, the fast-paced Dekhni and slow-n-gentle Mando
- *Feni –* local Goan liquor made out of coconut toddy or cashew fruit juice
- *Pedd –*a circular podium/pedestal to sit, around the banyan tree, a holy tree
- *Taluka –* a division of a district
- *Taii-* **or** *Tai -*(Konkani/Marathi) -AHindu elder sister
- *Xacuti-* a Goan curry dish of grated coconut, red chili, onion and spices
- *Zatra or Jatra -* a pilgrimage festival celebrated at a Hindu temple (also known as *yatra* in India)
- *Papal bull –* Pope's decree/s conferring a right to colonize, convert and rule the colonies (originally given to Spain and Portugal*)*

Old Conquests: The mainly western costal districts of Goa: Bardez, Ilhas, Mormugão, Salcete and Old Goa (the first capital) that the Portuguese had conquered until it acquired seven more districts in the north, east and south between 1764-1788 known as the New Conquests.

www.ingramcontent.com/pod-product-compliance
Lightning Source LLC
Chambersburg PA
CBHW051223130726
47988CB00001B/203